"Betsy Kandell, known as Tuffy in her numerous camp sojourns, is off this year to camp Ma-Sha-Na and a whole new bunch of bunk mates. Always on top of a situation, effervescent Tuffy loses no time in psyching out her cabin partners (from boy-crazy Natalie to quiet, sensitive Iris) and learning the lay of campland, all of which Angell relates through peppery, upbeat dialogue." —*Booklist*

"Ms. Angell exhibits a flair for humor as well as considerable knowledge of summer camp life."
—*Children's Book Review Service*

"Tuffy, in fact, is an impetuous, thoroughly likable camper. Her story abounds with life and is genuinely funny." —*Book World*

JUDIE ANGELL lives in South Salem, New York, with her musician husband and two sons. She has been an elementary school teacher, an editor for *TV Guide* in New York City, and for five years the continuity writer for Channel 13, New York's Educational Television Station.

THE BUFFALO NICKEL BLUES BAND, *Judie Angell*

DEAR LOLA OR HOW TO BUILD YOUR OWN FAMILY,
     Judie Angell

RONNIE AND ROSEY, *Judie Angell*

SECRET SELVES, *Judie Angell*

SUDS, *Judie Angell*

TINA GOGO, *Judie Angell*

WHAT'S BEST FOR YOU, *Judie Angell*

BLISSFUL JOY AND THE SATs, *Sheila Greenwald*

IT ALL BEGAN WITH JANE EYRE, *Sheila Greenwald*

WHERE HAS DEEDIE WOOSTER BEEN ALL THESE
     YEARS?, *Anita Jacobs*

IN
SUMMERTIME
IT'S TUFFY

by Judie Angell

LAUREL-LEAF BOOKS bring together under a single imprint outstanding works of fiction and non-fiction particularly suitable for young adult readers, both in and out of the classroom. Charles F. Reasoner, Professor Emeritus of Children's Literature and Reading, New York University, is consultant to this series.

Published by
Dell Publishing Co., Inc.
1 Dag Hammarskjold Plaza
New York, New York 10017

Laurel-Leaf Library ® TM 766734, Dell Publishing Co., Inc.

ISBN: 0-440-94051-6

RL: 4.9

Reprinted by arrangement with Bradbury Press, Inc.
May 1979
10
WFH

For Dick

1

"Mo-om! I'm home! MOM?" We live in a four-room apartment but sometimes I can't find my mother.

I walked into the hall and zoomed right in on a folded brochure sitting next to the phone. At that minute there wasn't anything else in the apartment but that brochure. It's like in the movies, when they want to get your attention . . . The camera gets closer and closer to something until that's all you can see, like the pair of glasses the murderer left on the table, or the monster's hand moving when he's not supposed to be alive.

BOATING! SWIMMING! TENNIS!
PARADISE ON EARTH

For youngsters from five to fourteen!

CAMP MA-SHA-NA
in beautiful Honesdale, Pennsylvania!

Camp. Another camp brochure.

"*Mom!*"

I took the brochure into the kitchen and poured myself some milk. I was halfway through the second glass when Mom appeared.

"Hi, Betsy, I didn't hear you come in. How was school?"

"Fine. What's with this?"

"The camp brochure? That's where you'll be going this summer. How about a snack?"

"Okay." She started rummaging through the shelf. "How come you're doing this now?" I asked, "I mean, it's only February."

"Honey, you know we always have to sign up early for camp. The good ones are already filled by spring. Gee, I don't have any cookies . . . How about some sardines?"

"Yuck, no. Is this a two-month sleepaway camp?"

"Well, of course! How about some Chunky Soup?"

"No, I just had milk. Got any crackers?"

"Ah! Maybe." She started pulling out boxes. "Bets, why don't you *read* that brochure. I think you'll find it interesting. Noo-oo, no crackers. How about a macaroni-and-pimento salad? I think I have some lettuce—"

"Nah, forget it." I looked at a picture of Camp Ma-Sha-Na's lake. It was huge. But maybe that was just the way they made it look in the picture. "Hey, where's Jeannie?"

Mom was putting back all the boxes and cans.

"Napping," she answered. "She ought to be up in a minute. Feel like taking her for a walk later?"

"Not really. It's freezing outside." I started getting that weird feeling in my stomach . . . You know, like just before you get on the Cyclone at Coney Island. You know it's supposed to be fun, and it is, but still you're really scared. It's very strange not to know where you're going to be spending two whole months of your life. I'm eleven now and this will be my fourth summer of going to camp . . . It'll also be my fourth camp.

"Mom?"

"Hm?"

"How come I'm not going back to Camp Running Brook?"

Mom sat down with a plate full of macaroni-and-pimento salad. "Camp Running Brook was lovely, dear, but you didn't learn to swim. Did you see the picture of that lake?"

"Yeah. Definitely bigger than Camp Running Brook's. But last year you said you wanted a camp that stressed music and art, and Camp Running Brook was up to here in music and art."

"*This* camp stresses music and art, but they also promise you'll pass your Intermediate Swim Test before the end of the summer."

On the back page was a picture of Camp Ma-Sha-Na's tennis courts. Actually, I don't like tennis. The racket's always too heavy for me, and I hate to get all sweaty. "Well, I passed my Beginner's Test at Camp Wyndale, remember? How come I didn't go back there?"

"Betsy, Camp Wyndale had Color War. I'm not sending you to another camp that encourages such fierce competition."

"MAAAAAAA!"

It was Jeannie. She always yells like that when she wakes up. I don't know how she does it. I can't even speak when I wake up. Mom dropped a forkful of pimento and ran out to get her. She always likes to get Jeannie to the bathroom *immediately*; otherwise, it's too late. We've been trying to toilet-train Jeannie for about a year-and-a-half. I have a theory that she really knows what to do . . . It's just her thing not to do it. I mean, she's *not* a baby, she's almost three.

Actually, my sister is kind of the reason I began going to camp in the first place. Mom got pregnant when I was seven and she had to carry through the summer, which she said was the *worst* time. Anyway, she thought it would be better for all of us if I spent the summer at camp. Also she said she wanted to get me out of a hot apartment on Long Island.

I picked up the brochure and went into the bathroom where Mom was holding Jeannie up on the toilet so she wouldn't fall in. "You know," I said, "this camp sounds okay. It has porches."

"It has what?" Mom asked.

"Porches on the cabins . . . a place to sit."

"Oh! Fine. Listen, I forgot to tell you—JEANNIE, DON'T SLIDE OFF! I forgot to mention that Natalie Zinser and Adele Brody will probably be going with you to Camp Ma-Sha-Na. Their mothers wanted me to call when I checked on all the material."

I sat down on the edge of the tub. "Why aren't they going back to Camp Running Brook?"

"Well, their parents felt—JEANNIE, GET YOUR HAND OUT OF THERE! They felt that the physical activities left something to be desired. Also, Natalie came home with her ears pierced, and Adele didn't get a tan."

"Are you going to call them now?"

"I thought I'd get to it after dinner."

"Can I call them now?"

"Okay, but when I talk to their mothers, you watch Jeannie on the seat."

I ran to the phone book. I decided to call Nat first.

Natalie is absolutely not like me at all. She's very mature for her age, which is almost thirteen. She's very tall and has a waist. And she has long, dark straight hair. I once tried to iron my hair to look like Natalie's, but I set the iron on cotton instead of synthetics and my hair all burned and turned white. I had to have it all cut off and now it just sits on top of my head and looks like some little kid's drawing of hair.

Natalie answered the phone. "Hello."

"Natalie? It's Betsy."

"Who?"

"Betsy Kandell . . . From Camp Running Brook."

"Tuffy?"

"Yeah."

"Oh, hi!"

"Hi!"

"Well, how are things in West Hempstead?"

"Good. How's Great Neck?"

"Boring."

"Sorry. Listen, my mother said we'll be going to camp together again . . . this summer. A different one. This one has a really big lake, and *two* tennis courts."

"How far is the boys' camp?" asked Nat.

"Gee, I don't know. And guess what? It has porches on the cabins in the pictures!"

"What?"

"Porches! You can sit outside, even when it rains!"

"Well, is the boys' camp part of the girls', or is it across the lake or something?"

"I didn't see. Listen, they've got canoes and sailboats—"

"Tuffy," said Natalie, "do you have that stuff there about the camp?"

"Yeah, right here."

"Well, look it up . . . About the boys' camp and what ages they go to."

"Just a minute." I thumbed through the pages. There was a fold-out I hadn't seen before. It was a map of the camp. "Nat?"

"Well?"

"It looks like the boys' bunks are on the same side of the lake, if that's what these little boxes mean. The girls are on one side of the Rec Hall and the boys are on the other. And the brochure says 'youngsters from five to fourteen'."

"Oh. Fourteen? Well, they'll have older counselors and waiters."

"Listen, Natalie, my mother wants to tell your mother about it. Is she there?"

"Yeah, I'll get her. Tuf?"

"What?"

"Are you going to call yourself 'Tuffy' again this year?"

"Sure, it's on all my name tapes."

"You know, you'll really have a better time with the boys if you stop being 'Tuffy'."

"I had a great time with the boys! Remember the raid I led on the last night with Bobby Bruner?"

"I didn't mean that kind of time, Tuf. You're a year older now. You'll be twelve soon. There are other things you do with boys at camp besides go on raids. Are you learning to dance this winter?"

"Natalie, I can't dance. I'm a clod."

"I'll teach you, I promise. Tuffy, don't embarrass me this summer."

"I won't, Natalie. You won't have to go on raids if you don't want to. Hold on . . . MOM!" No answer. I told Nat to wait and went to look for Mom. She was not in the bathroom anymore. "MOM?"

A muffled yell, "Wha?"

"Natalie Zinser's mother is coming to the phone. Where are you?"

"In the bedroom closet. Tell her I'll call her back."

I told her, and hung up. Last summer Natalie spent all her time hanging around Ronnie the Waiter, who *had* to be eight years older than she

was. He wouldn't even look at her. Once he pulled
her hair. She was thrilled. Yuck!

My name is really Elizabeth. It's a great name,
because you can do so much with it. I was Liza for
about two weeks last year . . . After Liza Minnelli.
Then I was Beth, and then Betty for about six
months after that. Mom and Dad call me Betsy.
And my teacher, Miss Chandler, calls me Liz or
Lizzie, because that's what she calls her own
daughter, Elizabeth. I haven't decided who I really
am yet. In the summer I like "Tuffy," because that's
who I am then.

I looked up Adele's number. She lives in Great
Neck too. She and Natalie go to the same school,
but she's a year younger than Nat, like me. Adele
is also short like me, and she has frizzy hair too.
But it looks good on her. She's very pretty, actually, but she has terrible allergies and her nose is
always red.

Her brother, Arnold, answered the phone. He
was at Running Brook too.

"Hi, Tuffy!"

"Hi, Arnold! We're going to a different camp
this summer."

"We are? What's the name of it?"

"Ma-Sha-Na . . . It's in Pennsylvania."

"I'm going to put a frog in your bed the first
night, Tuf!"

"I'm gonna bury all your underwear, Arnold.
Put your sister on." Last year Arnold was nine, and
a pest.

Adele got right on. "Hi! Arnold says we're going to camp together again. Great!"

"Natalie, too."

"Good. Hey, I'm a cheerleader for the Eighth Grade Basketball Team this year!"

"Neat. We don't have cheerleaders. West Hempstead has Junior Ramettes."

"Junior *what?*"

"Ramettes! See, the name of the team is the Rams, so the Ramettes are a bunch of girls who are like a chorus line and kick their way around the basketball court."

"During the game?"

"I don't know. I haven't been to any games."

"Oh."

"Listen, my mother wants to talk to your mother. Can you hold on a minute . . . MOM!" No answer. I went to look. "MOM? Adele's mother is on the phone."

"Tell her I'll call back . . . The spaghetti's boiling over!" Mom yelled.

I told Adele. "Okay," she said. "See you in four months!"

It'll be fun to be with Adele. I wonder if her nose gets réd in the winter too, or just in the summer.

Four months.

Maybe porches on cabins are a good omen.

2

Dr. Barber is our pediatrician. I've always loved his name. It's like he never really decided what he wanted to be when he grew up, a doctor or a barber. Doctor . . . barber. Eeny . . . meeny. When I'm sitting around in his waiting room I always play these games . . . Like if his last name was Dentist, and his first name was Barber, then he'd be Doctor Barber Dentist. Or if his last name was Electrician and his middle name was Dentist, then—

"SO, it's Betsy Kandell, here for another camp check-up!"

"Hi, Dr. Barber!"

"AND Sylvia! How *are* you?" He held out his hand to Mom, but she was busy pulling Jeannie off the receptionist.

"Hello, Howard. Yes, we're here for Betsy's physical. I have all the forms here somewhere—"

She started taking stuff out of her purse and piling it on the receptionist's desk.

"WELL, you find them," said Dr. Barber, "and then just come on into the office. Meanwhile, Betsy and I will have a little chat."

I followed him in and sat down on the chair next to his desk. It was a plain straight chair. His was one of those that swivel around and let you lean all the way back, so I just sat and watched him swivel and lean.

"WELL, Betsy, (lean) how's school this year?" (swivel)

"Fine."

"Let's see, it's, uh, sixth grade now, right?" (swivel)

"Right."

"And (lean) what is your favorite subject?" He always asks the same questions every year.

"English, I guess." And I always give the same answers.

Mom opened the door. "Howard, I think I've found everything." She came in, followed by Jeannie, who looked around, saw how boring the room was, and scooted right out again. "Well," Mom said, "I guess she'll be all right in the waiting room. Now, let's see . . . Here's the form for special medication requirements."

"I don't need special medication, Mom," I said.

"I know that, honey, but you have to send the form in anyway."

"Blank?"

"No, with a bunch of 'No's' and 'Okay's' on it."

Dr. Barber took all the forms from Mom and put them on his desk. "WELL, Betsy, let's have a look at you. How's Dave, Sylvia?"

"Just fine, thanks, Howard. Not much time for golf these days, though." Mom sat down, and we both watched Dr. Barber unwrap his examining tools.

"I know, I haven't seen him recently." He began to look in my ears with his pointed light. "AND, Betsy, what do you like to do after school?"

This was the question I've always hated. Nobody ever expects you to say, "I like to watch *Another World*." I shrugged.

"Extra-curricular activities? Sports?" he asked shining the light in my eye.

I coughed. "My throat," I said.

"Hm?"

"My throat . . . You forgot to examine my throat."

"JUST getting to it," he said, picking up one of those wooden things. Blagh! Why did I remind him? Those wooden things always make me gag.

"SO, what was it you said you did after school?" Since I still had the stick down my throat, I gargled at him. I guess he took that for an answer because he dropped the subject.

Actually, at our school the big after-school thing *is* sports, but the wrong ones for me. The popular sports are gymnastics or handball or paddle tennis. I like baseball and football okay. But most of the time the boys don't let me play. Anyway, that's why camp isn't so bad . . . There's a lot to do besides sports.

Dr. Barber tapped my knee with his hammer and my left leg flew up and kicked him. "Mmmm, your reflexes are fine." He kept writing things on the form. "AND is it a different camp again this year, Betsy?"

"Yup."

That was the only hard part. Each year a new place 'til Mom found The Perfect Camp. But when I really think about it, the newness doesn't last all that long. Living with people, you really get to know them pretty fast . . . And the camp routine, too. It's just the waiting 'til you get through the beginning that's always bothered me.

WOW, that stethoscope was cold! You'd think that doctors would have figured out a way to warm them up by this time . . . maybe store them in a bowl of warm water.

"And now," said Dr. Barber, "I guess that just about completes it. Have a very good time at camp, Betsy."

"Thank you, but I don't leave until July. This is only April."

"Well, honey," said Mom, collecting her stuff, "Dr. Barber won't be seeing you again before. That is, unless you get sick . . . And you're not going to do that!"

"Well, I hadn't planned on it." None of my camps were in Pennsylvania before. Mom said Honesdale was in the Poconos. I've seen some commercials for vacations in the Poconos. But you can't tell anything from commercials.

We walked out of the office, and I went to pull Jeannie off the receptionist while Mom said goodbye to Dr. Barber. What if his last name was Management Consultant?

When Daddy got home from the office that night, I went over the camp brochure with him again. "The cabins look really pretty in the pictures, don't they, Daddy?"

"They do, Bets. I'm sure you're going to have a wonderful time. Those porches are a nice feature."

"I think so too. Daddy?"

"Hm?"

"Did you ever leave home for a long time when you were young?"

"No, honey," he said. "Grandma and Grandpa couldn't afford to send me to camp. You're a lot luckier than I was."

3

The morning we left for Camp Ma-Sha-Na was the first time in four summers that I didn't throw up before we got in the car. Actually, we almost missed the camp bus because everybody was waiting around for me to do it.

Mom came into my room with my comb and brush. "Betsy, have you packed everything? Are you all right?"

"I'm all right so far. No, everything's here on my bed because you said you'd get my overnight bag down from your closet shelf, remember?"

"Oh, yes. Now let's see . . . Got your toothbrush . . . Here's your comb and hairbrush . . . What about your vitamins?"

"They're in the refrigerator. Mom, I need soap, toothpaste, shampoo and hair conditioner."

Mom said, "Doesn't the camp supply those things?"

"Well, you can buy them at the canteen, but it doesn't open 'til the second week."

"Oh, well, we'll stop at a drug store on the way. Now what else do you need, dear?"

"I think I have everything . . . My favorite shirt that I didn't want to send ahead, my jacks, my tennis racket . . . How about my lunch?"

Mom looked worried. "Are you all right? Are you sure you're all right?"

"I am, I am. Did you pack me a lunch?"

"Yes, I did it last night so I wouldn't forget. Now can you think of anything else?"

"Yes, Mom, my overnight bag."

One thing that's always the same on camp-leaving day is the New York Port Authority Bus Terminal. I guess it can't be helped, but it is really scary if you don't know what to expect . . . And is still is, even if you *do* know what to expect. That's because it seems like every camp in America is leaving from there on the same day. You see a zillion kids and two zillion parents. The kids all look kind of funny, like every one of *them* threw up before they got in the car.

I started looking for the big banner on a long pole that had my camp's name on it. But when you're really short, all you see are a lot of shoulders and heads and tennis rackets, which all the kids carry because you can't pack those. Finally, after shoving and pushing for about a year, I heard Daddy yell, "Found it, Bets! Over here! Just follow the seven-foot overnight bag!"

I saw him swinging my blue bag over his head and kind of scrunched toward it, like a quarterback sneak, until I caught up with him. "Boy, lucky Mom decided to stay in the car with Jeannie! This place is wall-to-wall people!"

Daddy said, "It sure is. How do you feel?"

"Fine, fine. Do you see a sign that says Junior Girls Bunk Ten?"

Daddy looked around. Good thing he's tall. "Got it! See that pillar over there on your left? Well, there's a sign on it. Let's move over that way."

We got there, finally. The counselor, whose cardboard name tag said "Sheila" on it, smiled at me and asked me my name. "Kandell," I said.

She pulled out a name tag from her tote bag and handed it to me saying, "Hi, I'm Sheila," which I already knew.

My name tag said "Elizabeth Kandell." I put down my stuff. "Daddy, can I use your pen?"

"Sure, Bets."

I turned the name tag over and wrote in big capital letters, TUFFY KANDELL. You have to get these things straight right from the beginning.

Daddy turned to Sheila and held out his hand, "Hi, Sheila, I'm Dave Kandell."

"Hi, Mr. Kandell."

"Is this your first summer at Camp Ma-Sha-Na?" he asked her.

Sheila smiled, "It's my first summer at any camp, Mr. Kandell. I never even went as a camper before."

Daddy said, "Well, don't worry. You'll have a great summer." I gave Daddy back his pen. "And," he added, "you have a terrific kid in your bunk to help you start out right!"

Everybody smiled and I elbowed Daddy. "I'll be okay now, Dad. You can go."

"You sure?"

"Yup."

"All right, honey. Have a wonderful time. We'll see you on Parents' Weekend. And Betsy, don't forget to write *often*. So long, Sheila, have fun!" I watched him move into the crowd.

There really wasn't any reason for him to stay. I mean, I'm practically twelve years old, and I'd found the group I was supposed to be with, so how would it look for my *father* to be standing around with me.

I looked up and found one of the Junior Girls squinting at me. She was trying to read my name tag. Hers said "Debbie Kern."

"Tuffy?"

"What?"

"No, I mean is that your name?"

"It's a name tag, isn't it?"

"Well, yeah, I mean it's just—different."

She said "different," not "dumb." That was a good sign. I don't like kids to be afraid of me, exactly, but I don't want them to think they can push me around, either. And I like to get a kind of picture in my head of each kid in my bunk as soon as I can, so I know what to expect for the summer.

Debbie asked, "How many are there supposed to be in our bunk?"

"Six, I think. I know two of them from last summer, but they're not here yet."

"Oh, three of you already know each other?"

"Don't worry about it. In camp everybody gets to know each other very quickly. After all, you live together. Can I see your tennis racket?" Maybe some day I'll meet a tennis racket I can live with. She handed it to me. Naturally, it was too heavy.

"What have you got for lunch?" she asked.

I hadn't looked, but I figured it wasn't very much. Since I usually throw up, Mom probably got nervous and didn't pack a lot. I was right. "Tuna fish and a Yodel."

"Hey," she asked, "Wanna jelly donut for the Yodel?"

I took the Yodel out of my bag and gave it to her, but I let her keep the jelly donut. *Nothing* gets soggier than a jelly donut on a four-hour bus ride in the summer. Just then I felt a tap on my shoulder, "Hi, Tuf! You wrote that name tag yourself."

"Hey, hi, Natalie! Wow, you look great! I see you haven't cut your hair. Oh, this is Debbie."

"Hi."

"Hi."

"Hey, where's Adele?" I asked. "Didn't you guys drive in together?"

"We did, but she forgot her allergy pills, so she and her mother went to find a drug store. Arnold's here somewhere, though."

"Goody. Where are your parents?"

"Oh, I sent them away as soon as I saw you. Are we the only ones here?"

We all looked around. One girl I hadn't noticed was sitting against the pillar on her overnight bag. She was reading a heavy-looking book. I didn't see anyone else, and the group right next to ours was Senior Boys. We kept staring at the girl 'til she took her eyes off her book and looked up. Debbie squinted at her name tag.

"Hey, what's that say?"

"My tag? Iris Connor."

Debbie said, "Hi, Iris. I'm Debbie. This is Natalie and this is, uh, Tuffy."

Iris didn't bat an eye at my name. She nodded and said, "Hello," and went right on reading. I had to know what was keeping her so busy that she didn't even feel like talking to the people she'd be living with for eight weeks. I walked around to the back of the pillar to sneak a look at the book. I figured I could do it casually enough, since she was sitting down. It didn't work, though; I was too short. Sitting down, her head was blocking my view of her lap; so I had to either lean left or right. I did both several times until I realized I must look pretty dumb, bobbing around like that, and I still couldn't see anything. Finally, I remember a trick that the kids in school use when they cheat on tests. They either drop their pencils next to the smart kid's desk and then lean way over to pick them up, or else they re-tie their shoes while staring at the paper on the desk in front of them. Since I had no reason to be using a pencil, the shoe idea was better. I untied both my sneakers and bent down right next to Iris's book. While I was tying them, I looked at the pages. There were funny little diagrams on them, and a picture of a weird-looking guy with a beard and a pointy hat standing in the middle of a circle. Written on the circle were strange words and some Roman numerals.

"Do you mind?"

I looked up into Iris's face.

"Your head is in my way," she said, "and I can't read."

"Oh, hey, I'm sorry," I said. How come it works for the kids in school? I stood up quickly. "Uh, Iris, I just wanted to see the name of it . . . The book, I mean, because you seem so interested in it." Great way to start a friendship, being totally embarrassed.

Iris didn't seem to care. She flipped over the cover . . . *A History of Conjuring and Magic.* Jeez! "Oh, terrific," I said, and moved back to the group. Okay, it was a weird book, but if she didn't make a smart remark about my name then what she liked to read was all right with me.

I saw Natalie with her chin up in the air. That meant she was checking out every boy in the Port Authority Terminal. She keeps her head up like that because they have to be at least six inches taller than she is or she's not interested. "Look, Natalie." I nudged her. "Those are the Senior Boys."

"For gosh sakes, don't *point* at them!" she

hissed. "Besides, I'm not interested in Senior Boys. They're only fourteen. I want to look over the waiters, and I'm sure they're already up there."

Suddenly I felt a poke in the back. It was Adele's tennis racket. She was trying to put on the name tag Sheila had given her. "Hi, Adele! How are ya? Did you get your medicine?" I asked.

"No-o!" she wailed. "We couldn't get a prescription. My doctor wasn't home when we called. I think his son leaves for camp today to. In fact, he's probably here. I've been looking for him."

"What camp?"

"Who knows? Just get ready for me to be miserable the second the bus passes the Bronx. Hi, Nat! Who is everybody?"

We introduced her to Debbie and Iris just as the last Junior Girl arrived. Her name tag said "Verna D. Perkins." Debbie squinted at it. Verna said, "That's a terrible squint. I used to do that, but now I have reading glasses."

"What's the 'D.' for?" Debbie asked.

"It's not for anything yet. I can pick whatever name I want when I'm sixteen, as long as it starts with a D." The tall lady with her put her hands on Verna's shoulders and kissed her cheek.

"Goodbye, dear. I hope all of you girls have a marvelous summer."

"Thanks, Mom. 'Bye." Verna looked like she was going to cry. She didn't though.

All of a sudden there was a lot of movement. Some of the camps were beginning to move toward the buses, and you could hear all the counselors' whistles blowing. There were so many whistles you didn't know where to look, but Sheila kind of herded us together and told us to follow her big bunk sign. At last.

Iris Connor was in front of me. She had an overnight bag and a tennis racket, like the rest of us, but oh, wow, she also had a guitar!

4

Music and magic . . . Those were two hobbies nobody in West Hempstead had, at least that *I* knew. I decided to sit next to Iris on the bus and wait for her to tell me about them or maybe play her guitar. I waited . . . And I waited. After the first hour-and-a-half, the only thing she said was, "Would you please put my left-over lunch up on the shelf over the seat, since you're on the outside." And she just went on reading that book. This time, though, I was able to read some of it without getting in her way:

> "Incantations that brought out spirits were comprised of holy names, spoken in a mixture of Hebrew, Latin and sheer gibberish, and they usually ended with a command spoken in plain language."

What did *that* mean? Sheer gibberish was right. What if Iris was a witch? If Iris was a witch, it was definitely better to be her friend than not.

"Iris?"

"Hm?"

"I saw your guitar. I think it's neat that you can play. What kind of music do you like?"

"All kinds," was the answer, and she never looked up from the book.

"Iris?"

"What?" Finally she turned toward me.

"Uh, where do you go to school?"

Back to the book, "I go to private school . . . In Westchester."

"Do you study this?" I asked, touching the book, "in your school?"

She clicked her tongue at me, "No."

"Have you ever been to Ma-Sha-Na before?" I asked.

"No. One other camp, not this one."

"I've never been here, either. Uh, did both your parents bring you to the terminal?"

"No, they're in Europe. Our housekeeper brought me."

"Oh." This was really not my idea of a great conversation. In my head I made up a list of other possible things to bring up that might take Iris's head out of that book. If we were going to spend a whole summer together in the same bunk, I wanted to know what she was like. Why didn't she want to know what I was like? Let's see, I thought: School was out . . . Music didn't make it . . . Magic I didn't understand . . . I could ask her if she has any brothers or sisters or what she does after school. No, I'd sound just like Dr. Barber.

The bus began to slow down. I sat up and looked out the window. We had arrived at the Red Apple Rest. It's a big roadside restaurant where practically all the camp buses stop so the kids can go to the bathroom and buy a drink or something. Two of my other camps stopped there. I thought about whether I wanted a drink, and remembered I hadn't even eaten my tuna fish sandwich yet.

"Oh, thag God," said Adele, staggering to her feet. She had a faceful of tissues and her eyes were watery. "I've GOT to get a box of Kleenex." She knocked against Debbie who was the first one off the bus. Iris didn't look like she was going to move.

"Aren't you going in?" I asked her as I stood up.

"No, I'll just sit here and read," she said.

"Well, you want me to bring something back for you?"

"No, thanks."

Natalie and I got off together and followed the mob into the restaurant. There were three other camp buses already parked, and another one just pulling in. I thought I'd buy a coke, but I still wasn't hungry.

I saw Adele picking up a whole armful of pocket-Kleenex packages and went over to help her. "Oh, Tuffy, I'b so BIZ-erable," she wheezed.

"Well, don't worry," I said. "As soon as we get to camp, we'll get you your medicine. Just hang on."

GROAN, from Adele.

"Hi, Adele!" Both of us turned around. There was a tall boy smiling down at Adele.

"Greg!" Adele growled. "Great! Where were you whed I deeded you?"

"Huh?" said Greg.

"I was lookig all over the terbidal for you ad your father," she said.

"Why?"

"Because I forgot by prescription ad I ca'd breathe, *that's why!*"

Greg looked at me. "Are you her doctor's son?" I asked.

"Yeah."

"Well, I'll translate for her. She can't breathe because she forgot the prescription for her allergies, and she was hoping she'd run into you before your father left the terminal. She's mad because seeing you now doesn't do her any good."

"Uh, oh! Well, have a good summer, Adele," he said and went back to his group.

Adele groaned, "Thags, Greg. I'll have a wudderful subber."

I looked at the lines waiting to buy drinks and they were miles long. I decided not to bother, and went back to the bus. Debbie was already back, poking into a brown paper bag.

"What did you buy?" I asked.

"Oh, they didn't have any good candy," she said, "so I got popcorn. But it's stale."

"Well, don't eat it then."

"Are you kidding?"

I took out my tuna fish and it looked terrible . . . all mashed together and soggy. "What's that?" Debbie asked.

"A yucky tuna fish sandwich."

"You mean you haven't eaten it yet? God, aren't you starved?"

"No, I'm really not."

She looked at me and then at the sandwich.

"Debbie, you want this thing?"

"Well, you can't let it go to waste. And if you wait any longer it'll just get worse," she answered.

I handed it over and sat down. Iris was turning pages like crazy. What a boring trip!

The singing started as soon as everybody got back on the bus. First it was "Ninety-Nine Bottles of Beer on the Wall", which some counselor insisted on singing all the way down to one bottle. Then it was "Row, Row, Row Your Boat", followed by "I've Been Workin' on the Railroad." Iris didn't offer to play her guitar, and by the time they got around to "Home on the Range" I decided it was time for a nap.

The thing about naps is you're really hungry when you wake up from them. I was starved. But it was about two o'clock when we got to camp so, naturally, no food 'til dinner.

Natalie checked out right away where the boys' bunks were. The girls were all in a row on a hill above a big open field called the Quadrangle. All my camps have had a Quadrangle with a flagpole in the middle. That's where the camp meets before breakfast and dinner for flag-raising and lowering. The boys' bunks were in back of the Rec Hall, spread out in the woods, and you couldn't see them from the road. The Rec Hall is really the

Recreation Hall, and that's where they put on plays and have dances and movies and things. The other big building in most camps is the Mess Hall, and, of course, that's where everybody eats. I've found that camps all have the same buildings . . . They just put them in different places and paint them different colors.

Junior Girls Bunk Ten was the first bunk in the row, but the one farthest away from the Rec Hall, which bugged Natalie because it was the farthest away from the boys. And, it meant we had to drag our stuff farther than the other girls, too.

"Okay," Sheila said, as we got to the porch, "your trunks and duffle bags are already in there, so pick out your cots and start unpacking. Let's get that over with!"

We looked around our new home. The porch ran the whole length of the bunk and it had a log railing all around it. The bunk was wood, white-washed on the outside, but plain on the inside. And there was only a screen door on the front.

"There's only a screen door!" Verna cried. "Anybody can see us when the light's on!"

"So what?" said Natalie.

"Don't worry, Verna," Sheila said quickly. "We'll put up a draw curtain right over the door and we can just pull it closed at night."

Verna whined, "But what about *tonight?*"

"We'll improvise with a sheet, okay? Don't get upset, just find your stuff. Everyone find a bed."

In the one big room there were seven beds, four on one side and three on the other. The counselor always has the bed next to the door. I don't know why. In case anybody sneaks in at night, she gets it first, I guess. At the far end of the room, in the middle, there was a door to the john. We suddenly all decided we had to use it at once, but there were only two toilets so we all hopped around until everyone had a turn. There were also two old sinks with rusted pipes underneath and a crooked tin shower.

"There's no shower curtain," Verna wailed.

"Don't worry," Sheila said, "we'll use a—"

"SHEET!" Natalie screamed, and we all broke up. "There'll be nothing left on our beds by the time Verna's through covering herself up!"

"Come on, come on," Sheila called, "don't tease Verna. There's nothing wrong with a little modesty. Now, is anyone's trunk missing?"

Luckily, no one's was. I picked out a bed next to Sheila's and pulled my trunk over to it. And then I picked up Iris's guitar and put it on the bed next to mine. She looked at me. "Okay?" I asked.

"Sure," she said and pulled over her own trunk.

Adele had flopped on the first cot she saw and was writhing around. Sheila ran over to her. "Oh, poor baby, you're really in a bad way. We'd better get you to the infirmary. But I don't know where it is!"

"I'll find it, I'll go with her," I said.

"Good, Tuffy," said Sheila, "I'm going to have to supervise the unpacking, so that would be nice if you'd take her."

Adele had used up her Kleenex packages so we

got her a wad of toilet paper, and the two of us went out to find the infirmary. There were some counselors wandering around the Quad and they told us where it was. They were probably the Specialty Counselors, like the Drama Counselor and the Swim Instructor, because usually they don't have to be in charge of a bunk of kids. Adele kept falling on her knees every two minutes, praying that they'd have her pills. "I'b gudda die if they do'd give me subthig," she moaned.

The doctor practically had the prescription waiting. I guess he was used to allergy problems in camp. I sat around reading the eye chart until Adele felt better, and when she finally got herself together we decided to explore instead of going back to boring unpacking.

"Gee, it only took four hours to get here," Adele said. "Last year it took about seven."

"That's because Camp Running Brook was in Maine. This is in the Poconos. It's a lot closer to New York."

"Well, it's a good thing," she said, "because I never would have made it to Maine."

"Oh, hey!" I yelled. "Look at the lake!"

We had come to the top of a grassy hill in back of the woods that hid the boys' bunks. Down at the bottom of it was a lake you couldn't see the end of. There was a dirt path that led down to the swimming area and the dock. The dock was huge and shaped like a H. Most camp docks are shaped like that. The kids who can't swim play in the inside of the H, where they can walk in and out of the water. After you pass your tests, you can swim in the outer H and go out to the float. We walked down, sat on the dock, took off our sneakers, and hung our feet over the edge.

"They'll kill us for being down here without a counselor," Adele said.

"We won't stay long. Look how big it is!"

"Yeah."

"Remember last year, Adele? You could row across *that* lake only taking your oars out of the water once. A lake this size means they really mean business about teaching you to swim."

"I guess so." Adele was sliding down farther and farther, trying to get as much of herself wet as she could. "Oh, this water feels so good. Hey, Tuf, do you remember Uncle Al?"

"The Head Counselor at Running Brook?"

"Yeah! Remember the fit he had the last morning of camp when you sneaked in and put the Bill Cosby record on the P.A. system instead of reveille?"

"And the whole camp woke up to 'Hey Hey Hey, Fat Albert', and he thought it was a deliberate joke about him?"

"It *was!*"

We started laughing and Adele fell off the dock. I jumped in after her and it was a lot of fun, except I forgot to take off my Mickey Mouse watch. Anyway, we were nice and cool when we climbed back up the hill.

Both of us stopped suddenly as we got near the bunk, Adele said, "You know, we're really late."

"And wet," I added.

"Oh boy, we're gonna get it."

"They really hate it when you go near the water-front without a counselor." That was always a big camp taboo.

"Yeah." Neither of us moved. "Hey, do you think we could borrow some dry clothes from someone before we go back?"

"Good idea, Adele, except we don't *know* anybody; our hair is dripping wet; and Sheila knows what clothes we left in."

"Right," Adele said. We just stood there, squishing our sneakers. "Well, what do you think they'll do?"

"Maybe they'll stop the buses before they leave and send us back to Port Authority in disgrace."

"Okay, Tuffy, you're so brave, let's go and face it."

"Okay," I said, and neither of us took a step.

"I'm getting cold," Adele said.

"Me, too."

"Well?"

"In a minute."

Finally, Adele started ahead of me. "I'm going, Tuffy. If I catch a cold now, I'll never know which are my allergies and which is the cold. I'll be taking so many pills they'll probably cancel each other out and *then* where will I be?" And there she was, on the porch, pulling open the screen door. Verna was putting on shorts and screamed. "It's okay, it's only us," Adele said. "We're, uh, a little wet."

Debbie said, "Hey, don't drip on my leather jacket!"

"All right," said Sheila, coming out of the john. "What happened to you two?"

"Well—" Adele began.

"See, Sheila, while we were outside, there was this real crazy rainstorm, just came out of nowhere! You probably didn't notice, being busy unpacking and everything, but—"

Sheila threw us a couple of towels.

"How do you feel now, Adele?" she asked. "I almost forgot why you left! You sure look a lot better."

"Oh, I am," said Adele. "They're going to keep pills for me at the infirmary and I have to go there to take them after breakfast every morning."

"Good. Now how about changing into something dry and unpacking your stuff?"

I looked over at Sheila while I was peeling off my wet stuff. She had forgotten us already, and was busy hanging up a bathrobe. No yelling, no punishment! Good beginning!

5

Unpacking is my least favorite thing next to math, field hockey and Brussels sprouts. I hate folding stuff and putting it away, because it always works out that whatever I need is way in the back and under something. I opened my trunk and started piling stuff on my bed. When my father packs for me, I can just take it from the trunk and put it right on the shelf. But when I pack myself, forget it.

I looked at Verna's and Iris's beds. They each had neat little piles of clothes all ready to be put away . . . Tee-shirts in one pile, jeans all folded, blouses on hangers, shorts together, everything organized. I tried to copy them by at least putting the same things together, even if I couldn't fold like they could, and started stacking stuff on the shelves of my cubby.

Cubbies are what they call the things you keep your clothes in, I don't know where they got that name. They're really just wooden boxes nailed up on the wall with some shelves built in and then a long space underneath for hanging things. Usually the kids get to decorate their own cubby doors.

Debbie wasn't bothering with organization. She reached into her trunk, pulled something out, and tossed it right into her open cubby. Then she started getting cute, tossing a shirt over her shoulder and a pair of underpants under her left leg.

"Debbie!" screeched Verna.

"What?"

"That's terrible! That's no way to unpack. How will you ever find anything?"

"Well, I'll just throw out things until I find what I want, and then I'll throw them back again. What's the big deal?"

Verna looked like she was going to faint. "But everything will be all wrinkled and squashed!"

"So what?" Debbie asked. "It's only jeans and tee-shirts and stuff. I mean, there's nothing here for the prom."

"Would you just let me help you?" Verna was over at her bed folding by this time. "I mean, Debbie, we are seven people in a small bunk. I just can't live in a mess!"

"Yeah, I can see that," Debbie said.

"We're all going to have to cooperate or it'll just be impossible," Verna was saying as she stacked shorts and folded socks. Poor Debbie, I thought, the first time she has to get clothes out of there and wrecks Verna's patterns.

Leaning down for my duffle bag, I saw Nat's

cubby was packed solid. But when I looked at her bed, there was another cubbyful sitting on it. Nat had just changed into a pair of shorts and a peasant blouse. "Natalie, what's all that stuff?" I asked.

"My second trunk," she said. "Gee, these cubbies are small."

"They're small if you have two trunks."

"I happen to have a lot of clothes," Nat said, "and it's silly to have them and not wear them."

"It's silly to have them, period," Debbie said. "How many pairs of jeans do you need? I mean, if you tear them, then you *patch* them; you don't change them!"

"Clothes," said Natalie, getting annoyed, "are one of my hobbies. I know all about fabric and color and what looks good on me. Clothes are not something just to put on your body to keep out the weather!" She turned to Debbie, who was counting her tee-shirts, "Will you *please* get your hands out of my things?"

"How are you going to sleep," I asked, "with your hobby all over your bed?"

Sheila stopped her own unpacking and came over to Natalie's bed, stepping over shoe boxes and open trunks. "Nat, there's just too much stuff here for your cubby. Are you sure you want it all?"

"Yes."

"Why don't we all chip in a shelf of our own for Nat?" Adele asked. "Looks like none of us needs all the shelves we have, anyway."

"I don't want anyone else's things in my cubby," said Verna.

"Wait a minute," Sheila said, "Natalie, why don't you pick out the things you think you'll need the least and put them back in your trunk. Then, instead of storing your trunk with the others, we'll just keep it under your bed. How does that sound?"

"Oh, fine," Nat said, smiling at last. "Great, that's what I'll do."

"I don't think it'll fit under the bed," I said, looking at the height of Nat's trunk.

"No, you're right," Sheila said, measuring the height with her hands.

"Why don't we use it as a coffee table?" Nat said.

"A *coffee* table?" Adele asked.

"Well, that's what they call them. You know, those tables they have in living rooms that you put magazines on and things. We could just put it in the middle of the floor."

"If we put it in the middle of the floor," Debbie said, "we'll have to leap over it every time we want to go to the john. And when I have to go to the john, I don't want to leap!"

"Look, this is getting silly," Sheila said. "We'll keep the trunk on the porch, against the bunk wall. It won't get rained on, and if Nat needs something she can just step out and get it. And that's enough about Nat's clothes, okay?"

Everyone went back to what she was doing . . . Nat dragged her trunk out to the porch; Iris took out her magic book; Sheila wrote a letter; and I just stood around starving.

Finally, the bugle blew back-to-the-bunk.

Thank God, I thought, almost dinner! The bugle record sounded wavy. Must've been stored next to the furnace all winter.

The back-to-the-bunk call means that wherever you are in the camp you're supposed to go back and change into long pants for dinner, because it really gets cold in the mountains at night. And after that you still have some time for Free Play or quiet games in the bunk or something. Then the bugle blows another call while they lower the flag, and the Head Counselor usually makes announcements.

Since it was the first day and practically everybody was already back at the bunk, all we had to do was change to warmer clothes. This was my third change of clothes today and I was getting bored, so I just kept on my tee-shirt that had my name in cartoon letters on the front and back, and tied a sweater around my waist. Then we all sat on our beds and watched Natalie put on a pair of maroon slacks, a pair of French jeans and a pair of green corduroys before she decided on white ducks.

Suddenly, Verna leaped off her bed. "The sheet! Sheila, we forgot the *sheet!*"

"What sheet? Oh, you mean to cover the door. Okay," Sheila said, getting up, "anyone want to volunteer a sheet?"

We all looked at Verna. "All right, all right." Verna said, going to her cubby. She took out a sheet and a box of pins, needles and thread. "We need a curtain rod," she said.

"How about a bent hanger?" Adele offered.

"Well, how will we put it up?" Verna asked.

Iris put down her book and was looking at the door. "How about resting it on two nails sticking out on either side of the door frame? You could wrap thread around the ends of the hanger and then around the nails to hold it."

Since Iris hardly said anything all day, we just stared at her before anyone did anything. She went back to her book.

"Oh, great!" I said. "Terrific idea! Do we have any nails?"

"Pull some out of the walls," said Nat. "Look, there's one." There were some rusty nails sticking out of the wall over some of the beds that some kids must have hung things on. We pulled out the straightest ones and Sheila hammered them up on each side over the door with her wooden-wedge shoe. Then Verna, using the pins like curtain rings, pinned the sheet to the hanger so it could slide back and forth. We all thought it was the dumbest thing we ever saw. Natalie said maybe we should tie-dye it. And just then the Line-Up call blew.

The Head Counselor's name was Uncle Otto. That's how he introduced himself to the camp after the flag came down. He had a very deep voice and he said he wanted us all to call him Uncle Otto. He was a really wide person, and he came out to Line-Up in baggy green shorts with a white stripe down the sides and a white tee-shirt that had CAMP MA-SHA-NA—STAFF written across the front of it in green-painted leaves.

After he had made himself a member of all our families, he made a little speech.

"I want to welcome you all to Camp Ma-SHA-Na," he boomed. "We have many wonderful activities planned for each and every group, and we want this to be a summer you will all look back upon with fond memories. Now many of you have probably wondered about the origin of our camp's name—"

Debbie whispered, "Were you wondering?"

"Not really," Natalie said.

Uncle Otto went on: "Perhaps you thought the name was taken from the famous Indian tribe that roamed this part of the Pocono Mountains many years ago—"

"That's it," Verna said.

"But that is not the case," Uncle Otto continued. "Perhaps you thought it came from the name of the great river that feeds our beautiful lake. Or you might have assumed it was an Indian word that described some natural wonder."

Iris yawned.

"No, counselors and boys and girls, none of these is the answer. Camp Ma-SHA-Na got its name because its original owner named it after his three children, Marvin, Shari, and Nancy."

The whole camp groaned. And he went on, "I wish you all a healthy, safe, and happy summer. We're now going into the Mess Hall to have a fine dinner and later our Evening Activity will be Camp Introductions."

Dinner was shock time for Natalie. Camp Ma-Sha-Na didn't have any waiters in the Mess Hall. The bunk counselor was supposed to get the food at the window and bring it back to the table for everybody. After dinner, two kids were assigned to clear the dishes and bring them back to the window. Poor Nat! The waiters were the only reason she ever went to meals.

"My mother didn't say there were no waiters," she complained.

"Maybe there are dishwashers," I said.

"Dishwashers are *men!*" she explained, except I didn't get it. "Waiters are high school boys . . . Sometimes even college boys . . . They're on their summer vacation and they go to camp to meet girls."

"Twelve-year-old girls?"

"I'm almost thirteen, and I could pass for sixteen. Tuffy, if I'm bored with this camp I'm gonna blame it on you!"

I figured that Natalie was a little jealous of Iris because she kept staring at her all through dinner. Nat is usually the prettiest girl wherever she goes. She says so. Not nasty, I mean, she just knows it, and it's true. But Iris was going to be competition for her. She had the same kind of long, straight hair that Nat had, only hers was blonde. And she had a waist and a couple of other things Natalie didn't have yet.

"Where are the potatoes?" Sheila asked.

"Down at Debbie's end," said Adele. "How about the rolls?"

"Wow, we've got rolls!" I said.

"Sure, it's the first day," Natalie said. "This is your standard first-night dinner. We won't see rolls again until Parents' Weekend."

"The chicken's good," said Verna.

"Chicken you'll see plenty of," Nat said. ". . . In fricassee, pot pie, salad and soup."

"Please pass the salt," Iris said.

After dinner we went to the Rec Hall for Introductions. Camps always do that the first night and it's usually a big bore because everybody tells his name and where he's from, and nobody talks loud enough, and nobody remembers anyone the next morning. But Camp Ma-Sha-Na did it differently. They just introduced the Bunk Counselors, the Specialty Counselors and the doctor and nurse. And then we sang folk songs. Three people played guitars. One was a counselor named Paul, and when he finished singing, "Michael, Row Your Boat Ashore" Natalie said she didn't care about the camp having no waiters any more. Adele said, "Natalie, he's got to be *twenty!*" I kept my sweater off because I didn't want to cover my name on my shirt, but nobody said anything about it.

On the way back to the bunk I saw Natalie walking all alone behind us. Her whole face had changed. I could see that even in the dim lights from the flashlights.

"Nat?" Her eyes were all glassy. "Nat, what's the matter?"

"Tuffy, don't you think he's terrific?"

"Paul? He's okay, but that other guy played better guitar."

"Don't you think he's gorgeous?" she said, looking up at the sky.

"Well, he's awfully old, Natalie."

"Tuffy, you are a child!" She walked away from me toward Iris.

I caught up to them. Nat was saying, "Iris, that was a guitar case you brought up to camp, right?"

"That's right," Iris answered.

"Well, um, do you play?" Nat went on. No, Nat, I thought, she just carries a case around instead of a purse.

"Yes," said Iris.

"Well, look, Iris, do you think you could teach me? I mean, just enough to play maybe one song marvelously well. What do you think? Just a little, I mean. Could you?"

Iris turned to look at her but didn't stop walking. "I could show you a few chords," she said.

"Now?" Nat asked.

"Now? You mean tonight?"

"As soon as we get back to the bunk. Please, Iris? I want to be able to play by tomorrow."

Adele and I both said, "Na-at!" But she made believe we weren't there.

As soon as we got into the bunk, Nat whipped out Iris's guitar case from its place between two beams of the bunk walls. She plunked it on Iris's bed and began fumbling with the clips.

"I'll open it," Iris said quietly. They both sat down, and Iris picked up the guitar. "What song do you want to learn?" she asked.

" 'Michael, Row Your Boat Ashore'," Nat said.

"What else?" Adele mumbled.

"All right, watch my fingering," Iris said, placing her fingers on the frets. "This is your first chord. You sing your first note, 'Michael,' and then you put your fingers here when you strum." She began to sing. We all stopped getting undressed to listen to her. She was really good. She sure had a pretty voice.

"Okay, let *me* do it," Nat said, not quite grabbing the guitar, but almost. "Where did you say the fingers were after 'Michael'?"

Iris took Nat's fingers and placed them. "Now strum," she said.

"OW!" Nat yelled.

"You strum *down*," said Iris, "not *up!*"

"Well, why didn't you tell me? Look, I broke my best nail!" Iris sighed, took the guitar, and put it back in the case. Nat got up from Iris's bed sucking her finger and whimpering. Well, I thought, if Natalie wanted Paul to notice her, it would have to be for her looks and personality. She just flunked the talent contest.

"Going out, Sheila?" Debbie asked, as we were all getting in bed.

"Nothing exciting," she answered, turning off the light. "Just a counselors' meeting in the Mess Hall."

"Will they have refreshments?" asked Debbie.

"Maybe," Sheila answered.

"Bring something back, okay?"

"Debbie, you'll be sound asleep when I come back."

"I know, but wake me up."

"Goodnight, Debbie. 'Night, girls."

" 'Night, Sheila," we answered as she slipped out through the sheet and screen door.

It's very nice at night when most of the camp is asleep. The crickets make terrific noises and the trees all move together and sometimes, in August, you can see the Northern Lights. Quietly, I got up and walked outside on the porch to think over the day. You sure can't do that at night in an apartment when you're three stories up.

I thought about Iris and how different she was. And I thought about Natalie and the way she likes boys. Then I thought . . . Maybe I'll like an older boy this summer. Not twenty though. Nat's going to waste all summer running after Paul-with-the-Guitar, and he's never going to look at her. That's what happened last year with Ronnie-the-Waiter. And I thought, maybe I'll even pass my Intermediate Swim Test this year. Maybe Sheila will tell me how to really straighten my hair. Maybe I'll get a waist!

Then I went back inside and *finally* threw up.

6

"*Everybody up! Chilly morning! Long pants! Sweaters! GET 'EM UP!*" What a way to wake up . . . Uncle Otto yelling at the camp. I wondered why he didn't play the reveille record on the P.A. system. Maybe he thought it was important to give a weather report besides getting us out of bed.

Nobody got up. Not even Verna! And she was the first one unpacked yesterday, and the first one out to Line-Up last night. I didn't think I'd make it at all, I was so tired. We were still in bed when Line-Up for Flag-Raising was called, and Uncle Otto had to leave everyone to knock on our door. We all jumped at the sound of his voice.

"Bunk Ten! I want you to understand that *EVERYONE* reports for Line-Up when the call is sounded. We keep on a regular schedule at Camp Ma-Sha-Na, and I will not have one bunk spoil it for the rest!"

"God, he has a loud voice," Nat said, pulling her pillow over her ears.

Debbie was at the window. "He has a megaphone. He screamed in here with a megaphone!"

"No wonder my head is throbbing," moaned Sheila, getting out of bed.

"He doesn't need a megaphone. His normal voice could uproot a tree," I grumbled.

"Come on, girls, please get up," Sheila said.

We all did. Verna was dressed first, and had her bed made before Nat could decide between the blue turtleneck with her jeans or the red V-neck. What she really wanted was her yellow crew neck but that was in her second trunk, and she didn't want to go out on the porch to get it in her pajamas, with the whole camp lined up around the flagpole. Not yet, anyway.

"Look," Sheila said, "we might have a problem. I have a hard time getting up in the morning, and if one of you doesn't get up first and wake me I'm going to be in a lot of trouble. Isn't there one early riser?"

"I'll be first," Verna said. "I brought my own alarm clock. I'm used to getting up to bugles in camp, not yelling. So I'll just set my alarm like I do for school and wake all of you."

"Great," Nat mumbled.

We got out of the bunk just as the whole camp was going into the Mess Hall for breakfast, and so we missed all of Uncle Otto's announcements.

He was waiting for us on the Quad. Last night he was the Jolly Green Giant but this morning he looked like a gross black cloud. He had a very large lower lip and it seemed like it flapped when he was mad.

"I don't want this to happen again, Bunk Ten, is that clear?" He still sounded like he was talking through a megaphone.

"Yes, Uncle Otto," Sheila said, as if she was four years old.

"Girls?"

"Yes, Uncle Otto," chanted the school choir.

"Good. Join the others. And remember that Clean-Up begins immediately after breakfast. You missed the announcements, so Sheila will tell you what was discussed at the counselor meeting about the way Clean-Up works."

"How does it work?" Debbie asked on our way into the Mess Hall.

"Everyone has a job," Sheila said, "and we have to make a Job Chart that we can rotate every morning. Before First Activity, he inspects the bunks and rates them with points from one to ten. Then on Sunday, he gives a pennant to the bunk with the most points."

"Sounds like military school," Debbie said.

"No, it's not bad," said Adele. "The jobs are easy, except the john. That's yucky."

"Only if you're all slobs," Sheila said.

Breakfast was a disaster. We weren't in such great moods to begin with, but then Sheila said we had to have hot cereal first. Natalie groaned, "I hate hot cereal. Why can't I just have toast? All I have at home is toast."

"Look," Sheila said, "one of the things they told

us at that counselors' meeting was that all campers have to start the day with hot cereal and then you can have the second course, like eggs or pancakes or whatever they're serving that day. But hot cereal first, that's the rule. Uncle Otto says it sticks to your ribs. And, please, girls, after this morning's beginning, you'd better darn well stuff your little faces before someone comes around and inspects the bowls."

"I'm just having toast," Nat said, "and that's it."

Debbie said she'd eat Nat's farina as well as her own, so we could send back seven clean bowls to the kitchen without having to dump one in somebody's shoe. Then it was my turn. The second course was eggs. I like hot cereal but I hate eggs.

"Tuffy, hold your nose and eat the eggs," Sheila said.

"My mother said I don't have to eat eggs if I don't want to. Besides, I'm allergic."

"I didn't get your note about that," Sheila said. "What note?"

"If you're allergic to anything, it's supposed to be in the medical form your doctor sends before camp starts. Nobody gave me any note for you."

"Oh," I said. "Well, I brought it with me. My doctor forgot to send it."

"Okay," said Sheila, "where is it?"

"Well, uh, remember when Adele and I fell in the lake? It was in my pocket and I lost it."

"Tuffy—"

"I'll dive for it the first time we have swim," I said.

Sheila sighed, "Tuffy, what happens when you eat eggs?"

"I break out in big red blotches and then I throw up. And usually I don't make it to the bathroom first."

Sheila leaned back in her chair. "Tuffy, I don't know if you really had a note. I know what I think but I won't take a chance. If you throw up in the Mess Hall you'll just call more attention to our already famous bunk. So skip the eggs and eat enough to get through the morning without fainting, okay?"

"Okay, thanks, Sheila. The eggs are powdered, anyway. You'll see."

"Just so you don't have to send anything back, I'll eat her eggs," Debbie said.

When we got back to the bunk, Verna pulled out some sewing scissors and we made a Job Chart. You make it with two wheels, a big one that has the jobs written on it and a little one that fits on top of the big one with all our names on it. Every morning you turn the little wheel once to the right, so each person has a turn at each job.

"Does anyone know where the broom is?" Iris asked. "I have 'sweep', but I can't find the broom."

"We don't *have* a broom," Verna said, looking around. "I don't see one."

"Well, calm down, Verna," Nat said, combing her hair. "Somehow we'll get through this crisis."

"Iris, as long as it's your job, why don't you go to the Head Counselor's shack and see if you can

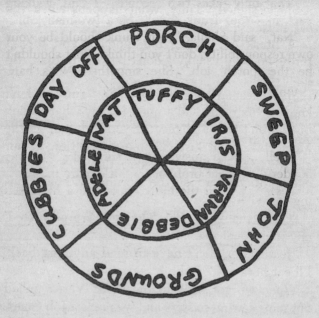

get our broom, okay?" Sheila said, and Iris took off.

I went out on the porch to make sure it was clean. Nat's trunk was open and a plaid shirt sleeve was hanging out of it.

"Now hear this," I yelled, holding my fist up like a megaphone. "From now on, whoever has 'porch' for her job will really be in charge of Natalie's Number Two Trunk! That'll be the only messy thing on it!"

Nat hollered through the screen, "It is not, Tuffy. The 'porch' job means checking for wet bathing suits on the railing and stuff like that!"

"That only takes two seconds," I said, walking back in. "Your trunk should be a two-man job!"

"Nat," said Sheila, "your trunk should be your own responsibility, don't you think? That shouldn't be the 'porch' job." She smoothed Nat's hair. "Come on."

"All right," Nat said.

"I've got 'grounds'," Debbie said. "How far around the bunk do I have to patrol?"

"Well," Sheila answered, looking like she was pondering a great problem, "a little more than two inches away from the bunk walls and a little less than an acre-and-a-half."

"Gotcha," Debbie said cheerfully, and she followed Nat outside.

Adele was poking into all the cubbies to straighten them. She got off easy since they were still pretty neat . . . even Debbie's.

Nat came back in, carrying the plaid shirt, "Will this be too hot to wear for the morning?" she asked.

"Natalie, what's your job?" Adele wanted to know.

" 'Day off'," Nat said.

"How'd you manage that?"

"It was my stationery you made the job chart out of, remember?"

The only one who really worked was Verna. She got right down on her hands and knees to scrub out the john.

"Look at her! She loves it!" said Nat. "I think she brought her own Brillo."

Iris came back with a broom and did a fast sweep. We were lying on our beds when there was a knock on the screen.

"Good morning, Bunk Ten."

Sheila jumped up. "Hi, Louise. Girls, this is Aunt Louise, Uncle Otto's wife." Aunt Louise would absolutely never win a contest called "Pick Uncle Otto's Wife Out of a Crowd." She was just the opposite of him . . . very thin and little with long black braids.

"Girls, I'll be bringing around your weekly schedule of activities every Monday morning for you to post next to the Job Chart," she said. "Here's the one for this week, and while I'm here I'll do this morning's inspection." Verna posted the schedule which we all ran to look at, completely fencing in Aunt Louise. "Uh, girls, would you mind—" she elbowed her way out and began peering around the bunk. "Dust on the floor, girls," she sang. "I can't bounce a coin on these beds."

"Military school," muttered Debbie.

"Try and tighten them up, all right? Oh, my, the john is beautiful!"

"Bonnie Brillo did it all herself."

"Natalie!" Sheila warned.

"Well," Aunt Louise said, "I'll have to take two points off for the floor and the beds, but you get an eight. See you next Monday." Nobody paid any attention.

Adele was looking at the schedule. "We have tennis first," she said, "then Arts and Crafts."

"Music after that," said Iris, quietly.

"Will you bring your guitar to Music?" I asked her.

"Oh, maybe, but not the first time," she answered, and went off to get her tennis racket as the bugle blew the end of Clean-Up.

The Tennis Counselor put me against Debbie, who turned out to be fantastic. For all she eats, she can really run. I couldn't hit one ball back to her. She kept hollering instructions, like "Tuffy, hold your racket higher! HIGHER! It's not golf!"

"Listen, I can't hold it at all. It's too heavy! I happen to be a small person!"

"Bend your KNEES, Tuf! You're too stiff!"

"Let's get a drink."

"Get BACK, Tuf, further BACK!"

I'd had it. "Hey, Debbie, I won't feel at all bad if you want to play somebody else. Honest. Play Natalie. She's good."

"Oh, okay, but how're you going to learn anything?"

"From watching, Deb. I'm really watching."

Adele played Iris. Iris was even better than Debbie and she hardly looked like she was sweating. She floated around the court. "Hey, Iris," I called, walking over to her as she was towelling off. "You play tennis really well. I mean, you look good running around after that silly ball."

She smiled. "Thanks," she said.

"Do you take tennis lessons in the winter?" I asked.

"Of course," she said, almost to herself.

"Of *course?*"

"I mean yes," she said. "Tennis lessons, music lessons, riding lessons and ballet." She walked away from me then and I couldn't ask her any more questions.

But right after lunch, during Rest Hour, I tried again.

"Iris, do you like all those lessons you take? Riding and ballet . . . and all that?"

"Why not?" was the answer, as she pulled out a book from her cubby. I guess she had finished the other book. This one was just as weird. Its name was *Spirits, Stars and Spells: The Profits and Perils of Magic.*

"What's that book about, Iris?" I had to ask.

"Uh, spirits, stars and spells."

"Are you a magician or something?"

"No, it's not about tricks. It's about real **magic.**"

"Do you believe in real magic?"

"It's a very interesting subject," was all she said.

During Free Play, our group decided to play volleyball and I went up to the Head Counselor's shack where they always keep all the equipment. No one was in the office, but the door was open and I went in. On the walls were rows of framed certificates. They all looked the same except for the dates, which started from 1955 right up to now, and the names of the camps on them. They all began "The N.C.A. Outstanding Director Award to Otto W. Sherman." I was checking out the small print when he stomped in and made me jump a mile.

"What are you doing?"

"Uh, getting a volleyball. It's okay, right? I mean, to come in and get equipment when we need it?"

"I see you are reading my award certificates."

"Yeah."

"You're in Bunk Ten, aren't you?"

"Uh huh."

"The ones who were late this morning."

What's the big deal, I thought. "Well, it was the first morning—"

"Young lady, I received all of those awards each year because of the kind of camp I run. I run a camp like a very tight ship. Every person must do his part or what we end up with is a sloppy operation. Running a camp is a big responsibility and it should be a constructive experience for everybody." I just looked at him. I couldn't believe this lecture I was getting. I didn't even *do* anything. I guess he didn't like the look, because he said, very evenly, "What is your name?"

I took a deep breath. "Tuffy."

"Tuffy. Well, Tuffy . . . *I* am tougher."

Dinner turned out to be hamburgers which, fortunately, everybody liked.

7

After dinner we all walked over to the volleyball court where we had left the ball. Except Iris . . . She said she wanted to go back to the bunk to write a letter. We were waiting for Evening Activity which was going to be a movie, "Mighty Joe Young." It's about a gorilla; I've seen it about forty times on T.V.

I picked up the ball and threw it to Nat. "I got the ball, you guys, so someone else takes it back!"

Nat tossed it to Debbie. "Here, Deb! Take it back."

Debbie wrinkled her nose at the ball and lobbed it over to Verna, "You go, Verna."

"No, you go, Adele," Verna said and rolled it to her.

"Tuf?" Adele said, as I was about to get it back.

"No, come on, that's not fair," I said. "I was the one who got it. What's with you, anyway?"

"I'm exhausted," Nat said, and sat down on the grass.

"Poor Nat. It's all that clothes-changing," Debbie said. "It really knocks one out!" Natalie ignored her.

"I don't want to go to the H.C. shack," Adele said. "Uncle Otto makes me nervous. Even when he talks normally, he thunders."

"That's why I don't want to go," Debbie said.

"Me too," added Verna.

"Well," I said, "he was in there when I went to get the ball and it wasn't too bad." Debbie and Verna looked at each other and then started back to the bunk.

"What do you mean, it wasn't too bad?" Adele asked as she threw the ball to me.

"I mean, I just acted pretty cool and told him what I was doing there and there wasn't much he could say. He even walked in on me while I was reading the stuff on his walls."

"What's on his walls?" Adele asked.

"Ten thousand awards for being the World's Meanest Head Counselor. And a row of shotguns, slingshots and bullwhips."

"I have to go to the infirmary," Adele muttered, and split.

Nat and I were left bouncing the volleyball back and forth. Then I got a terrific idea. "Natalie, you know the H.C. shack isn't far from the Rec Hall. Maybe Paul is up there practicing for the singing after the movie. Why don't you take the ball back and then you could stop off there and check it out?"

"Ooh, great idea! Let's have the ball!"

"Nah, on second thought, forget it. I'll take the

ball myself. You don't want to run into Uncle Otto."

"Tuffy!"

"Okay, okay! I'll tell Sheila so she'll know where you are and we'll meet you there."

Back at the bunk, Iris was lying on her bed writing her letter. Verna and Debbie were playing jacks.

"Hi, Iris."

"Hi."

"Want to play jacks?"

"No. No thanks."

" 'Go Fish'?"

"Uh uh."

"Poker? Gin Rummy?"

"No, I want to finish my letter."

"To your parents?"

"Yes."

Adele walked in then. "Hey, wanna play jacks with four?" she asked.

"Okay, but let's play with two sets," Debbie said. "It's harder."

"No, I have a better idea," I said. "Let's play Monopoly! I love Monopoly."

"No, Tuf," Adele said, "you cheat at Monopoly."

"I do not cheat! I just drive very hard bargains."

Debbie said, "You drive hard bargains? Like what?"

"Like if you land on my property and there are at least two hotels on it, you have to do my clean-up job for two days."

"Oh, no," Debbie said, "it depends on the property. I'll give you that deal for Boardwalk, but forget it if it's Illinois Avenue."

"No way. Two hotels are worth two days' clean-up."

"Tuffy, you play my kind of game! Fantastic!" Debbie said. "Who's got a set?"

"Arnold has one," said Adele.

"Great! I'll go over to the boys' camp and get it," I said.

The boys' campus was really different from ours. It was deep in the woods and dark. It was peaceful and nice. Ours was out in the open and you could see the main road and practically all the buildings, but the boys could hardly see to the next bunk. They didn't have porches though.

I saw a boy leaning against a tree chewing a weed. He didn't see me so I watched him. He didn't move. He just stood there, chewing his weed and looking at the trees. It would have made a nice photograph. His parents would like it. I went up to him, "Hi."

"Hmm."

"Do you know Arnold Brody?"

"Nope. What bunk is he in?"

"That's what I was going to ask you. I'm trying to find him."

"Well, how old is he?" asked the boy.

"Ten."

"Oh, that's Sophomore Boys, Bunk Four . . . Over there."

"What're you?" I asked him.

"What do you mean, what am I?"

"I mean, what bunk?"

"Senior Boys, Bunk Eight."

"Oh. See ya."

I was right. I thought he was a Senior Boy. I don't know why Natalie doesn't pick someone like that.

I found Arnold's bunk and yelled for him. He came outside.

"Hi, Tuf! Come on in, we're dressing for the movie."

"Big thrill, Arnold, watching a bunch of little kids taking off their clothes. Let me borrow your Monopoly set."

"Why should I?"

"Because if you don't I'm going to push your face in your farina tomorrow morning, Arnold."

"I'm not afraid of you," he said, but he went in and came out with the set.

"Thanks, Arnold." I grinned at him. "Your face is safe for another day!"

"Hey, Tuffy, how's my sister?" Arnold yelled as I was walking away.

"She's fine. Didn't you see her at dinner?"

"No, I mean, are her allergies bothering her?"

"She's okay, Arnold. You better watch it or I'll tell her you were worried about her."

"I'm not worried about her," he said, and slammed his door.

When I got back to the bunk, everyone was outside. "What's wrong?" I asked.

Iris said, "Sheila can't find Natalie and it's almost time for the movie."

"She's running around the camp looking for her," said Verna.

"Oh, jeez, I forgot to tell her!"

Just then Sheila came running toward us. She was practically crying. "I can't find her anywhere and it's getting dark. I'm supposed to know where all you girls are every minute. What am I going to do?" And then she *did* start crying.

"Sheila," I began, "I'm sorry; I'm *so* sorry. Nat's at the Rec Hall. She was returning the—" I stopped talking and Sheila stopped crying because at that moment we both noticed two silhouettes, one fat and one skinny, coming toward the bunk . . . Uncle Otto and Natalie. Oh, boy!

Under the porch light, Natalie was gray. She was cracking her knuckles, something she tells me not to do because it makes them ugly.

"Sheila, had you knowledge of the whereabouts of this camper?" His voice was very low.

Sheila said, "Uh—um—I—uh," and stopped.

And I said, "Oh, sure she knew. We all knew Nat was at the Rec Hall. She was going to meet us there, right?" No one answered.

Uncle Otto paid no attention. "Did you know that this camper was alone in the Rec Hall with a male counselor?"

Sheila looked at Natalie and then at me. Then she looked at Uncle Otto. "No," she replied, very softly.

"Bunk Ten, you are establishing a record for rule-breaking after only one day in this camp. I will not tolerate it. This camper," and he pointed at Nat, "is docked from tonight's activity and will remain in the bunk with a Junior Counselor, whom I will send over right now. Sheila, you are docked from your evening out after Taps and will remain with your group in the bunk." He turned and started to walk away.

"Wait a minute, wait a minute," I began. I felt he was being just so unfair. "Uncle Otto, we knew where Natalie was. She'd never take off without letting someone know. She, uh, knows all about movie projectors. Her father's a photographer, and she thought she could help get the films in order and set up and everything . . ." and oh, God, Natalie, say something, *please!*

"Yeah, right," from Natalie. "I always helped with the movies in my last camp. But the projectionist wasn't there, only Paul, and I was asking him about some folk songs."

Then Uncle Otto finished walking away.

Sheila said a strong word and then nobody said anything. We just stayed out there on the porch looking at each other until Marcia, a Junior Counselor, came over to babysit with Nat, who had turned from gray to red.

"Which one is Natalie?" Marcia asked.

"The red one," I mumbled.

"Huh?"

"I am." Nat said it firmly and quickly walked into the bunk, slamming the screen door and closing the sheet.

Marcia gave Sheila a quick look and followed Natalie inside.

"It's my fault," I whispered to Sheila as we all walked slowly toward the Rec Hall. "I told her I'd let you know where she was."

"It's okay, Tuffy, it would have happened anyway. She shouldn't have gone up there by herself when he's such a stickler for the rules. We sure are starting out badly, aren't we?"

"Well, at least not with each other," I answered.

Then we were at the door of the Rec Hall. Uncle Otto was standing right there staring at us because we seemed to be the last group to arrive. Inside I could see the whole camp, sitting in rows on those wooden benches waiting for "Mighty Joe Young." The lights were on and everyone was talking. And suddenly I totally shocked myself and everyone else! I don't know why I did it; I didn't plan it. But, out of nowhere, I put up both my arms and as loud as I could I said, "Listen, if our bunkmate can't come to the movie, then *none* of us comes! Come on, girls, we're going back to the bunk!"

Then it was like everything froze. I saw all the heads inside turn toward the door. I saw my bunkmates' heads turn toward *me*. Uncle Otto was looking from the rest of the camp to us. Sheila looked like she was about to collapse. And there was this truly terrible minute when I thought no one would move and I would have to crawl inside that Rec Hall. But it was beautiful! All six of us just quietly turned around and walked in the direction of our bunk and never looked back once.

There wasn't a sound coming from our bunk. We opened the door to find Natalie lying on her bed

staring at the roof. Marcia was on Sheila's bed
reading a book called *Hanging Loose in an Uptight
World*. She put the book down and stared at us.
"What are you doing back here?" she asked.

"It was a short movie," Debbie said.

"You can go now, Marcia, it's okay," Sheila said.
"We'll all be staying here."

"Well, but—" Marcia said.

"This happens to be a bunk problem," I said,
"for the bunk only."

"All right," Marcia said. She put her book under
her arm and left.

"What *are* you doing back here?" Nat asked,
sitting up.

"We missed your sweet face and sunny personality," I said.

"Oh," said Nat.

After the lights were out, I thought about the
scene at the Rec Hall. Where did I ever get the
nerve to do that? I wonder if I would have done
it if it was a movie I hadn't seen forty times on T.V.

8

Friday

Dear Mom and Dad,

This camp is okay. The kids in my bunk are nice.

I've had swimming lessons twice so far but luckily not for First Activity. Please ask Daddy to send me a pair of nose plugs because I hate it when the water goes up my nose. Have him do it, Mom, because remember last year when I asked you, you sent me ear plugs and a night mask.

We had Hike Day on Wednesday. That is the cook's day off, so everyone takes box lunches. We hiked to Colbrook River. You wouldn't believe how hot it was, and we had to wear long pants so we wouldn't get all bitten up. It was nice at the river. We couldn't swim in it because it was really a rushing mountain stream, but we waded and walked on the rocks. Verna fell in. She's this girl in our bunk who can't be happy until everything is neat and clean and organized. It's very hard for Verna because it's not just her own stuff she wants clean, but everyone else's, too. No one else cares.

We had an evening activity of indoor games in the Rec Hall one night. We played relays and dodge ball and stuff like that. We came in sixth in the whole camp when they added up all the points. I like movies better.

Right now we're going to a square dance so I have to stop writing. Yuck! I think I would rather have even indoor games than dancing. I will finish this after Taps with my flashlight under the covers.

I put my letter under my pillow and looked up to see Natalie making weird faces and holding her right earlobe with both hands. "What're you doing?" I asked.

"Trying—to—get—these—HOOPS—in—my—ears," she said between clenched teeth, as she squinted her eyes at the mirror.

"Hoops?"

"These. Look." She took away her hands and I saw a round gold earring, about the size of her palm. "I think the hole closed up since last summer."

"You mean where Donna pierced your ears . . . That time behind the boathouse?" I asked.

"Yeah! My mother wouldn't let me wear earrings all winter and now I think the hole's closed up. I'll have to have it re-done. OW!"

"Why wouldn't she let you wear earrings?" I wanted to know.

"I don't know; she has a thing about it." Nat was opening a small pink leather case.

"Now what?" I asked.

"Eye shadow and mascara," was the answer.

"Oh, Nat, come on," Adele said, "we're only going to a square dance. Besides, all you ever wore before was lipstick."

"That was last year, before I matured. A high school sophomore showed me how to do it. Look, you start here, at the corner of the eye, and then you swoop it up, like this, until you fill in the whole lid."

"Natalie, your eyes are all silver," I said. "They look like the hub caps on a Corvette!"

She frowned at me. "Grow up, Tuffy, and do something with your own face. It's dirty."

"Okay, I'll wash it. Anyway, no one else is putting on make-up, not even Sheila."

I went into the john and turned on the hot water faucet. Nothing! The cold water faucet let out a trickle of rusty liquid . . . Same with the other sink. Oh, well. I washed my face with the rusty water. It smelled awful. Looking in the cracked mirror over the sink, I wondered if we were going to get paired up with the boys or if we had to wait to get asked. Probably you got asked, and those that didn't get asked were paired up anyway so nobody got left out. I was always one of the ones that got paired up. When I didn't get paired up, I usually got Arnold.

"Come on, beauties," Sheila yelled. "Everybody out!"

Dear Mom and Dad (again),

I'm back. The square dance wasn't too bad. I danced the Virginia Reel with this Senior Boy. His name is Alex, and he's from East Flatbush. I met him the second day of camp when I was trying to find Adele's brother's bunk. Anyway, he didn't ask me to dance. We got paired up.

The food here is all right, but could you send my counselor a note saying I don't have to eat eggs, tomatoes or chipped beef. And please send me a salami from the deli in Lynbrook and a box of Mallomars. This is the longest letter I ever wrote. Don't expect to hear from me again for at least a week.

> Love,
> Your daughter,
> Tuffy

P.S. Is Jeannie toilet-trained yet?

9

It finally happened, the thing I always hate. Aunt Louise's new activity schedule had us down for swimming lessons, First Activity on Tuesday. We had two swimming lessons the first week, but they were both in the afternoon. It is SO AWFUL, swimming that early! Clean-Up is over at nine o'clock and you're still wearing your LONG PANTS because it's still freezing out! So right away you have to get out of all those layers of clothes and put on a bathing suit! I HATE HATE HATE IT!

"Sheila, what if I put on the bathing suit and then put my sweater and pants on over it?" I asked.

"Fine, but what do you do when you get down to the lake?"

"I'll worry about that then."

Debbie was already in her little two-piece thing and out on the porch. I was cold looking at her.

Natalie couldn't wait to put on her bikini that she keeps in a sandwich bag in her cubby. Absolutely nobody minded this but me!

I decided to settle for wearing a bathing suit and, over it, Verna's terry cloth robe that covered my toes. I wrapped myself up to my ears and tried to think "warm."

On the path down to the lake, Adele said, "Bet I can do the crawl out to the float without stopping once!"

"I can do that and swim back, too!" Nat said.

"Bet I can get my ankles wet without crying," I mumbled. But I didn't think so.

The Swim Instructor was a guy with a dog's name—Skipper. During lessons he always made you do the thing he was teaching you over and over until he liked the way you did it. That's okay, but at nine o'clock in the morning in a bunch of ice cold mountains, who needs it?

"All right, girls!" Skipper yelled. "Everybody jump in off the outer H and get wet! This morning we're going to practice the crawl, back and forth from one end of the dock to the other."

I sat down on the grass. The whole bunk was splashing around while I was busy arranging the robe to cover every part of my body except my head. Skipper stood on the dock facing away from the shore, watching them all swim, so he didn't notice me.

But Sheila did. I felt a soft kick on my back. "Tuffy, at least take off your robe."

"It's freezing."

"It's not. It's warm in the sun. In fact, it's getting hot. Come on, Tuffy, it's important for you to learn to swim. Please."

"Sheila, not for anyone else would I do this," I answered, unpeeling the robe.

"It isn't for *me*; it's for *you*. Go on!"

"Let me get wet in the *inner* 'H' first," I said, slowly walking to the edge of the water. I put in my toe. "YAHHHHHHGH!"

I shouldn't have screamed. It attracted Skipper's attention. "Tuffy! What are you doing over there? Come on, jump in over here."

"In a minute, in a minute! I'm getting wet first." Sure I was.

After fifteen minutes I was in up to my thighs. Also my wrists were wet. Just when I was deciding that MAYBE I could get entirely wet, a hard shove sent me right in over my head. I stood up, dripping, to see Debbie laughing. "*God'll get you for this, Debbie!*" I screamed. But I was finally wet, and I swam under the cross bar of the H to join the others. Once I got in, it wasn't too bad. The water was warm. The trick is not to let any part of your body hit the air!

Skipper was watching each girl do the crawl back and forth several times. It wasn't my turn yet. I began to play and really enjoy it. "Okay!" I hollered, "now I'm fine! What do you want me to do, Skipper?"

"Get out of the water. Activity's over."

"I'm glad we have Rest Hour," Debbie said, as we straggled into the bunk after lunch. "I get really tired about this time."

"It's all that eating," Nat said. "It really knocks one out."

"Fun-ny," Debbie said, lying down.

You don't have to sleep during Rest Hour, but you have to be quiet and rest for at least the first half hour. The mail comes around that time so you can read or write letters. Afterward you can play jacks or cards or sit on the porch. When Rest Hour is over, everyone walks out on the Quad for milk and cookies. Skinny kids have to have egg nog . . . Orders from the camp doctor.

Sheila usually sits outside on the porch the whole Rest Hour, writing letters to her boyfriend, Bob, who is a waiter in the Catskills. That's a summer resort area in New York. This time, all the girls fell asleep except me and Iris, who was playing "Bob

Dylan's Dream" on her guitar. I tiptoed out and sat down next to Sheila on the porch. Without looking up, she kind of slid her letter into her writing folder, but she did it slowly, so it wouldn't look like she was trying to hide it.

"Hey, I'm not interested in that love stuff, anyway, Sheila."

She smiled at me. "You'll write it yourself someday, Tuffy."

"Bleh!"

"You'll see. It's hard to be away from someone you care about." She looked up at the clouds, which were big and puffy, the kind you make imaginary pictures out of. "On one of my days off, Bob and I are going to hitchhike toward each other and meet in Narrowsburg. That's a town just over the Pennsylvania-New York border."

"Sheila," I asked, "how come you and Bob didn't work in the same place this summer?"

Sheila sighed. "Oh, lots of reasons. My parents thought we were seeing too much of each other. We go to the same college. I'm going to be a soph in the fall and he's going to be a junior. And he's working in a resort hotel. My parents think that's too unsupervised for me. Besides, he needs the money, and he can make a lot more at a hotel than in a camp."

Aunt Louise came by just then with the mail. Sheila got a letter from Bob, so she was *gone.* I took the rest of the mail inside. Iris looked up as I came in but she didn't stop playing. She was looking at the letters . . . Verna got two, Adele and

Debbie each got one and Natalie got two post-
cards, one from a boy named Harvey and one from
a boy named Ritchie. I didn't read them or anything, I just looked at the names on the bottom.
As I put the letters on the foot of each girl's bed,
Iris went on playing and began to sing softly to
herself.

I got a letter from Mom and Dad, but I felt a
little funny about reading it in front of Iris. She
hadn't gotten any mail yet, I was pretty sure, and
she was being so casual about it I knew it must
have been bugging her. I did my shoe-tying routine again so I could look at her face without seem-
ing too nosy. She didn't look at me at all, but
straight ahead of her at the opposite wall and went
on singing:

... How many a year has passed and gone,
Many a gamble has been lost and won
And many a road taken by many a first friend
And each one of them
I've never seen again.

I wish, I wish, I wish in vain
That we could sit simply in that room
   once again;
Ten thousand dollars at the drop of a hat
I'd give it all gladly
If our lives could be like that.

For the first time I felt badly that I got a letter.
I went out on the porch and sat on Trunk Number

Two before I opened it. Mom said they took Jeannie to Fire Island for a weekend to visit my aunt and uncle. They're both artists and have a summer house in The Pines where they do enormous murals. Mom said this summer my aunt is doing a red-and-black-squares mural and my uncle is working on one with tiny trees in front of large suns. Mom also said they'd probably have to bring Jeannie with them on Parents' Weekend because the baby-sitter they usually use when I'm away is going to be on a Meditation Retreat. Oh, well.

Iris changed the tune she'd been playing. I knew the song because I have it on a Peter, Paul and Mary album. It's called "Weep for Jamie" . . . Very sad and beautiful.

Sheila finished reading her letter for the fiftieth time and was smiling. I got up and went over to her. "Good letter, huh?"

"Mmm HMM."

I whispered, "Iris didn't get any mail again."

"Again?" Sheila frowned.

"Yeah."

Sheila bit her lower lip. "There's just no way to get in touch with her parents. They're traveling somewhere. Gee, I wish they'd write!"

I noticed the guitar music had stopped, so I figured I'd better change the subject. "Whaddya say we short-sheet Uncle Otto's bed tonight?" I asked.

Sheila laughed, "I know what that is. You take the top sheet and fold it in half under the blankets and when the person gets into bed, he can't put his feet down, right?"

"Right!"

"We do that at college," she said, smiling. Then she looked serious. "You know, speaking of Uncle Otto, he hasn't said a word about that night at 'Mighty Joe Young'."

"Why, do you think?"

Sheila didn't answer right away; she just looked at me. "I probably shouldn't say this to you, Tuf—"

"What? Tell me."

"I think he's not saying anything because he was really embarrassed. That's why he's willing to let the whole thing die."

I thought about it. "You mean, because we walked away before he had a chance to yell at us, or make us go into the Rec Hall?"

"I have a feeling he was too shocked to yell at us. We embarrassed him in front of the whole camp, especially you, because you're only a camper. Before he got himself together, we were halfway to the bunk. I just hope the whole thing is finished . . . the bad feeling, I mean. After all, he's my boss and your Head Counselor, and this is only the second week of camp."

"Well," I said, "we've actually been pretty good since then. Not late to Line-Up once and we even got a ten in inspection yesterday, right?"

Sheila put her writing stuff on her lap. "Right, you are all obedient, brilliant, adorable and *clean*. Now let me finish writing my letter."

I walked over to the screen door and looked in.

Iris was sleeping and her guitar had been put away. I went inside, trying not to squeak the door, and tiptoed to the row of cubbies. We had all decorated their doors over the weekend. I painted a lion's head on mine but it looked more cartoon then fierce. Natalie painted a red flower on hers with blue polka dots on each petal. Iris painted a silhouette of twin boys inside a black circle . . . She said that's her sign, Gemini.

I've always kept all my stationery and books under my dungarees in my cubby . . . also, the money Mom sends me for canteen. I took out my pen and stuff and sat down on Sheila's bed.

    Dear Mom and Dad,
      Surprise. It's only four days since I wrote you my last letter. I want to ask you something. A girl I like a lot doesn't get any mail from her parents because they are too busy traveling around Europe. She feels really bad and I was wondering, since you are not doing much traveling, can you write to her? Her name is Iris Connor, same bunk as mine.
      Please send me my catcher's mitt and my stuffed cat.

                    Love,
                    Your daughter,
                    Tuffy

"Tuf?"
"Hi, Deb."
"Rest Hour over yet?"

"Not yet. Go back to sleep."

She yawned, "I can't. Now I'm hungry."

"Debbie, you are *always*—"

"I know, but I can't help it. I'm a growing girl, and I burn up a lot of energy. Besides, I'm not fat, am I?"

"Stand up," I said.

She did and turned around.

"Well, no," I had to admit, "you're not fat. But you sure won't be on the doctor's list for egg nog."

"I know, and I really like egg nog, too. Oh, look, I got a letter." She picked it up. "It's from my sister in Michigan."

"I didn't know you had a sister," I said.

"Yeah, she's married . . . And pregnant. This letter's going to be all about her natural childbirth classes, just like my last two letters." Debbie read the letter and then looked up at me. "I was right. She and my brother-in-law are practicing breathing together. Wonderful! Why does she think that makes fascinating reading for a twelve-year-old?"

I shrugged, "I don't know. Why do you have to *practice* breathing? You do it all the time anyway."

"No, it's a special way you have to do it. Anyhow, it's boring. Want to play jacks?"

"Okay."

She took her jacks out of her sneaker. They were rolled up in a Milky Way wrapper. "Let's play for something," she said. "It'll make the game more interesting."

"What'll we play for?"

"Canteen money."

"Debbie," I warned, "I can beat you at jacks. In fact, I can beat you at any game that can be played sitting down. You'll be sorry if you bet your candy money."

"I feel lucky, Tuf. Play."

We played to see who would go first and I won. I went clear through sixties before missing. Debbie blew it on threesies. Then I got through tensies, walk-the-dog, and halfway through pigs-in-the-pen.

"Give up?" I asked.

"I can't afford to," she wailed.

"Well, this next one'll wipe you out."

"What is it?" she asked

"Rats-in-the-toilet," I said.

"Rats-in-the-toilet?"

"Yeah. You take your thumb and forefinger and put them together to make an O on the floor. Then you throw up the ball and you have to collect all the jacks in that circle; that's the toilet."

"Forget it, Tuf, I give up." She looked miserable. "I was saving for a Marathon Bar and a box of Jujubes. Now I don't even have enough for toothpaste."

"Debbie, you're breaking my heart. It's okay, I'll cancel your debt."

"You mean it?" she asked.

"Yeah. Hey, if you won, would you do the same for me?"

"Oh, sure, Tuffy, I'm really not allowed to play games for money."

"Me neither."

The bugle record blew for the end of Rest Hour. Everybody got to her feet and headed out to milktime on the Quad . . . Everybody except Iris.

"Iris?" I touched her shoulder.

"What?"

"Come on. Time to go. After milk we have Arts and Crafts."

"I'm coming," she answered. But I waited and made sure she got up.

When milktime was over, I asked, "Do you like Arts and Crafts? I mean, do you like to make stuff with your hands?"

"I guess so. I like to paint."

"Really? What kind of pictures?"

Iris thought. "I guess I like to paint whatever I'm feeling at the time."

What did *that* mean? "How do you *feel* like a table or a horse?" I asked.

"No, Tuffy," she said, rolling her eyes. "You paint a *feeling*. It doesn't have to be a *thing*, like a table or a horse. It doesn't have to look like anything in real life."

"Oh, I see. You mean like Picasso," I said. I thought, I'm not so dumb.

"Right," she said and smiled. "Look."

"At what?"

"At the Arts and Crafts shack. Right there, in the middle of those trees. It's very dark because of the woods, but look how the sunlight is so bright behind it. It's like there's darkness and sadness, but there's light and happiness right behind it. It's pretty, isn't it?"

I nodded. We stopped walking and looked at it.

I never would have noticed that. I mean, yesterday it was just the Arts and Crafts shack. Today, it's a picture of sadness and happiness; feelings. I decided it was time to start looking at things a little more carefully.

11

"I remember the diamond stitch but I can't remember how you do that square stitch that lets you move the lanyard up and down," Debbie said, winding yellow and blue plastic strings around a nail on the wall.

Barbara-Jean was the Arts and Crafts Counselor and she was showing everyone how to make lanyards, those colored, braided things you wear around your neck to hang a whistle from, or a ring or a key or something. Mostly their use is that they're just something to make in Arts and Crafts when the Arts and Crafts Counselor can't think of anything else. "It's a box stitch, Debbie," Barbara-Jean explained. "You take one color and bring it down, one over, one up, and one across . . . See?"

"No."

I finished my lanyard in two minutes and looked around to see what everyone else was doing.

"CHOO!" from Adele.

"Hey, didn't you take your pills this morning?" I asked.

"I forgot," Adele said, blowing her nose. "After breakfast Aunt Louise sent me around to all the girls' bunks for the B.M. charts and I never got to the infirmary."

"Well, why didn't you just take the charts to the infirmary in the first place?

"Aunt Louise wanted them first," Adele said, reaching for more tissues. Her half-finished lanyard was dangling from a nail in front of her. "Boy, that was dumb!"

"What? Aunt Louise getting first crack at the B.M. charts?"

"No, me forgetting my pills. Where's Sheila?" We both looked. She was outside, sitting on a rock, writing a letter. Iris was outside with an easel, painting.

"I'm going to tell Sheila I have to go to the infirmary," Adele said. "Wanna finish my lanyard?"

"Okay," I answered, sitting down in her place. Her lanyard was red and pink . . . to match her eyes and nose . . . Poor Adele.

"Tuffy, look at this!" It was Natalie, proudly holding up a thin bracelet made of lanyard material.

"Hey, that's nice, how'd you make it?"

"I wrapped the material around a flat piece of aluminum and then bent it to fit my wrist. Terrific, huh? What do you think it goes with?"

"Your mink stole," I answered.

"I don't have a mink stole. What about my purple tennis dress?"

"I love it," I said, as I finished Adele's lanyard and hung it around my neck with my own.

"Tuffy, what would you think if I made one for Paul . . . a very macho one, I mean, and gave it to him anonymously?" She was already picking out the flat piece of aluminum . . . a wider one than hers.

"You mean," I asked, "do I think he'll know which secret admirer it's from?"

"Yes. Do you think he'll guess?"

"Of course."

"Really?" she said. "How?"

"Because I'm sure you are constantly on his mind," I answered.

Natalie smiled. "Well, maybe not *constantly*," she said. "What do you think of brown, black and tan?"

"For Paul's bracelet you mean? Very macho."

"Good," she said as she began to sort out the colored strips of plastic.

I went out to see what Sheila was writing and Iris was painting. "Hi, Tuffy," Sheila said, licking an envelope.

"Hi. Letter to Bob?"

"Uh huh."

"How can you find so much to say every single day?" I wanted to know.

She looked down and smiled, "You just can. Did you finish your project?"

"Oh, yeah."

"What are the other girls doing? I know Adele went to the infirmary."

"Barbara-Jean is helping Debbie with her lanyard; Verna's working on her own! and Natalie is making secret gifts for the Maharajah."

"For Paul?"

"Yeah. Why don't you go in there and talk to her," I said. "She could give you some tips on how to make your man more interested in you."

"I'm sure she could," Sheila smiled. "Did you see Iris's painting, Tuffy?"

"Not yet."

"Well, go have a look. It's interesting."

Iris was working with her back to me, so I could look at the painting without disturbing her. She was using water colors—grays, blues, dark green and black. In the very front of the picture were two wheels, one large and one small. No, not wheels . . . Gears. They were gears, like in a watch, and she had painted them to look like they were turning and fitting together the way gears are supposed to. In the back of the picture was a girl . . . Or a woman, it was hard to tell. She had no clothes on and she was painted blue, almost in silhouette. She had a hammer in her hand, or a mallet, and she was pounding on a lever that was attached to a belt that looked like it made the gears turn. I thought about what Iris had said about painting feelings. But I didn't get a feeling like happiness or sadness from this picture she was working on. I didn't know what kind of feeling I got . . . anger, maybe.

One thing was definite. I would not ask her about the picture. I didn't want to interrupt her and, besides, I didn't want her to think I was dumb if I didn't get the right feeling from it. I'd just let her know I was there and tell her the picture was—interesting. I coughed softly so as not to startle her if she was really concentrating.

She turned around. "Hi."

"Hi, I see you're almost finished."

"Almost. You?"

"Oh, with the lanyard? Yeah. That's, um, really interesting," I nodded at the painting.

"Mmmm."

"Lotta dark colors," I said.

"Well, it's part of the mood," she said.

"Yeah," I said, chewing my thumbnail. "Uh, what mood?"

"The mood of the picture," Iris answered, and went on painting two more gears with broken teeth in the upper left-hand corner.

"Reminds me of a factory," I said, hoping it wasn't the wrong thing.

"Does it?" she asked.

"Well, the tools . . . Gears and hammers, and that belt—"

"Oh," she said, "I see what you mean."

Barbara-Jean came out of the Arts and Crafts shack. "There you are, Tuffy," she said. "Don't you have anything to do?"

"No, I've had it with lanyards," I said.

"Well, come on back in. Verna's enameling a copper pin. Maybe you'd like to make one. They come out very pretty. Oooh, Iris, let's see!" She peered over Iris's shoulder and stared into the picture, squinting her eyes. "Well," said Barbara-Jean . . . Iris didn't even turn around . . . "Well, such interesting colors." Iris still didn't turn around . . . "It's a beautifully constructed design, Iris."

"Thank you."

"Yes, wonderfully balanced," Barbara-Jean said. Iris nodded, and Barbara-Jean turned back to me. "Well, Tuffy, want to make something else? Verna will show you how to cut and mold the copper. I'm teaching Debbie the box stitch."

"Still?" I asked. Suddenly I saw Sheila jump up and put her stationery box behind the rock she had been sitting on. Uncle Otto was coming toward the shack.

"Hel-lo," Barbara-Jean sang.

"Hi," from Sheila.

"Good afternoon, everyone," said Uncle Otto. "I came to see how you were all doing and to check on the supplies, Barbara-Jean. Did the clay we ordered arrive?"

"No, not yet," she answered. "We're working with lanyard material and copper today."

"Well," he said, "I'll see about it. I want to see a lot of different projects developing here. The parents will enjoy seeing the variety of things our campers can produce." Out of the corner of his eye, he caught Iris's painting, looked away and, just as quickly, looked back.

"How nice," he said, walking over. "We have an artist. A real—" He stopped talking as he frowned at the picture. "Well," he said. Why did everyone say "Well"? Iris didn't turn around, and Uncle Otto backed away. He motioned for Barbara-Jean to come over to him and she did. I guess he thought he was talking quietly, but it's hard to turn such a deep voice down.

"That girl," he said, "Iris?" Barbara-Jean nodded. "She's, uh, quite good, I think."

"A fine sense of design," said Barbara-Jean.

"Yes, yes! Why dont you see if you can encourage her to paint something like a landscape . . . Some scene around camp. See if you can, will you? It would look nice in the Mess Hall."

I wondered if Iris had overheard that.

12

Dear Iris:

In case you find this typing sloppy, I must tell you that I am a housefly. And it's very difficult for a housefly to type, especially on a manual.

My name is Gikki and I live in a house in Groton, Connecticut. It's quite a lovely house and I have two rooms, a dining room and a kitchen. That's about all a fly can ask for. We don't need bedrooms and bathrooms like you *people*.

My only worry is flying into the web of Rikki, a rather nasty spider, who has been waiting for me for a long time. I can't imagine why, since there is plenty of food here for both of us, crepes Suzettes, asparagus Hollandaise, steak Diane and Buitoni frozen pizza. Yum! I assume you are enjoying such delicacies at camp, too. Isn't it nice we like the same things. I'll write you again if you like. Meanwhile, don't swat any flies in your sleep.

Love,
G.

The letter from Gikki cheered us all up, but especially Iris. I was sure it was her first mail. It made her laugh and she passed it around the bunk for the rest of us to see. She couldn't imagine who sent it. Good old Daddy! He's been sending me Gikki stories since I was little.

It was Friday and raining. We were all doing nothing but sitting around being bored. Natalie and Adele had gone up to the Rec Hall where some of the kids were playing Bingo and, of course, singing folk songs . . . which was why Natalie went.

Verna was taking off her shorts to put on a pair of heavy slacks and a big bulky sweater. "You look like Nanook of the North!" Debbie said.

"It's very damp in this bunk. I'm freezing. How can you all just sit around in tee-shirts and shorts?"

"It's not cold," I said, "just muggy." But she went on changing.

The screen door opened, the sheet was pulled back, the rain came in . . . And so did Arnold Brody.

"YAAAAAAAAAGH!" The blood-curdling scream came from Verna who, faster than a speeding bullet, fled into the john. Arnold froze in his tracks as her voice continued to beat on his head. "What's the *matter* with you! Don't you know you're supposed to *knock* when you come into a girls' bunk! Where were you brought up anyway! Where are your *manners!*" She was yelling all that between sobs and chokes. Meanwhile, Debbie had her face buried in her pillow to hide her shrieks of laughter; Sheila stifled giggles behind her hand and tried to read; Iris rolled over on her stomach so no one could see her face; and I screamed out loud. Poor Arnold just stood there.

"Is he *gone?*" Verna screamed from the john.

"Don't you dare say 'yes', Debbie," Sheila said, watching Debbie's face.

"I wasn't going to," Debbie said, but that devilish expression left her eyes.

Sheila got up and handed Verna's clothes into the john. A bare arm reached out and snatched them from her.

"Hi, Arnold," I said, "Adele's not here."

"Wh- What was *that?*" asked Arnold.

"That? That was our live-in maid. She's not used to people from the outside world. What do you want, anyway?"

"My Monopoly set. We want to play it in my bunk. There's nothing to do. It's pouring."

"I noticed." I got Arnold's game from Debbie's cubby where we had stored it.

"Adele's at the Rec Hall playing Bingo," I told him.

"I didn't come for her, I came for my Monopoly game," Arnold said on his way out.

"Arnold," Sheila called.

"What?"

"Next time, knock first!"

* * *

It stopped raining after dinner, just in time for Free Play. The sun came out a little, and there was even a rainbow. I love that time of day anyway and it's especially nice just after it rains, because everything is so shiny and wet and glistening.

I went down to the waterfront feeling pretty good. I was going to take a boat out by myself and watch the sun begin to go down. They let you do that during Free Play because Skipper is on duty down there along with a couple of Specialty Counselors. The only thing is you have to stay within sight of the dock. All the boats were taken except one canoe, and Alex, the dark boy from Brooklyn, was getting into it.

"Hi, Alex," I began.

"Hi."

"How come you're not playing baseball?"

"Because I'm going canoeing," he answered.

How could I talk him out of this canoe? "Listen, Alex, don't you want to go play some game? Canoeing is boring."

"It's good exercise," he said. "What's the matter with you, Tuffy? You want this canoe?"

"Yeah."

"Well, you want to come with me?"

"In the same canoe?"

"No, I thought I'd tow you in the water. Of *course* in the same canoe. You don't see another one, do you?"

"No, no. Fine, that'd be good." I quickly took off my sneakers and got in the front. He pushed us off from the shore and slid in the back.

Since I couldn't see him, I pretended I was in the canoe alone, only it was nice that he was there because it made the paddling a lot easier. I finally quit paddling and let him do it. He didn't seem to mind. In fact, he didn't say anything at all. When we hear the bugle blow back-to-the-bunk, I started to paddle again and we came back to shore.

"Thanks for the ride, Alex."

"Yeah, it was good exercise with the extra weight."

"Next time I'll paddle and you can ride," I offered.

"No way," he said and started up the hill.

Everyone was getting dressed for Evening Activity when I got back to the bunk, except Iris, who was reading *Spells and Potions*. Debbie walked behind her and squinted down at the page, "What're 'hove pations'?" she asked.

"That's 'love potions'," Iris said, looking up at her.

Verna shook her head. "You need glasses, Debbie."

"Iris, let's see that." Sheila was lying on her bed and reached out for the book. " 'Recipe for a Love Potion'," she read. "Is this for real?"

"Why not?" Iris shrugged.

Speaking of magic, Natalie appeared instantly next to Sheila on her bed. "Where's the recipe? Where? Where?" she blabbered, looking up and down the page.

"Calm down, Natalie, you're losing oxygen," Debbie said.

Sheila read out loud: "Tail of salamander, sprig of goldenrod—"

"*Goldenrod?* That let's me out," Adele said.

"Go on! Go on!" Nat said, shoving Sheila's arm.

Sheila went on: "Beetle scales, four drops pure rainwater, smatter of hens' teeth— What's a smatter?"

"Hens' teeth?" Nat cried. "How do you get *hens' teeth?*"

"How do you get 'tail of salamander'?" Debbie wanted to know.

"I can get *that;* I can get *that*. But hens' teeth—" Nat walked away, hitting her fist against her palm.

13

On Sunday morning at Line-Up, Uncle Otto gave the inspection awards to all the bunks. We stood there looking at our shoes while he boomed: "This week the pennant goes to *Bunk Thirteen*, with sixty-eight points!" The Senior Girls, Bunk Thirteen, cheered and yelled and thumbed their noses at the rest of the camp. "*Second* place—"

"Oh, jeez, what's he gonna do, go all the way down the line until he gets to us?" Debbie asked.

"That's how he gets his kicks," Nat said.

And he did . . . go all the way down the line until he got to next-to-last place, Bunk Ten. It drove Verna nuts. And that's when she started driving *us* nuts . . . On Monday morning, the third week of camp.

"Debbie, you didn't do your job."

"I did so, Verna, my job was 'sweep' and I swept."

"I just ran my hand along the floor and look!"

"Verna, what's with you?" Adele asked. "As soon as somebody walks on the floor you're going to have dust . . . Unless you want a little carpeting, or maybe an area rug."

But Verna wouldn't back off. "This bunk is going to win the pennant next Sunday if it's the last thing we do. From now on, *I'm* going to inspect before Uncle Otto, and we're going to show him what we can do."

Groans from everyone.

Verna went into the john. "Adele, there are tissues on the floor in here and the sink still has toothpaste on it. Yuck! What's this in the shower?"

"Oh, it's probably my hair coloring," Nat said.

"Hair coloring?" Sheila yelled. "Are you getting gray at twelve, Natalie?"

"No, actually, I thought I'd *add* a little gray," she answered. "I thought a streak, starting at the temple, would be sexy."

"Didn't the Bride of Frankenstein have a streak like that?" I asked.

"Fun-ny," from Nat.

"I don't care what it is, clean it up," said Verna. "Come on, girls, let's show some bunk spirit to the rest of the camp."

Iris went out on the porch to check it again. Nat rummaged around in the cubbies, folding stray clothes. It was my day off, but they all made me feel guilty doing all that work, so I went out to check the grounds with Verna. When Uncle Otto came around that morning, he was impressed. We could tell he was impressed because he didn't just glance around like he usually did and kind of mumble at us. He really examined everything carefully, and then wrote a "ten" on our inspection chart for Monday. We all cheered. Debbie gave Verna a box of Sno-Caps.

It was a great week. We got a ten in inspection every day but Friday, when we got a nine because Sheila had left her stationery box on the porch and nobody saw it . . . nobody but Uncle Otto.

Verna complained, "But it's a counselor! That's not fair! We shouldn't have to get points off when it's the counselor's fault!"

"I'm sorry," Sheila wailed, "I'm really so sorry."

"Oh, Sheila, don't be silly," Natalie said, "it's no big deal."

"Verna, stop making Sheila feel terrible," Adele said. "Besides, we can still win, I bet. No bunk has an absolutely perfect record." She went over and sat on Iris's bed. "Iris, play your guitar. Come on, please?"

"Oh, yeah," Debbie said, "especially for Adele play 'The St. James Infirmary'!"

"You want to sing?" Iris asked, opening the case.

We all wanted to sing. Iris played "The St. James Infirmary" and "Greensleeves" and "I'm in Love with a Big Blue Frog." It was a lot of fun.

But Saturday was really the best day. After lunch, Aunt Louise brought the mail as usual. Sheila took it around to each of our beds. There was a package for me from Mom, a post card for Natalie and a letter for Iris!

I watched her face. It was terrific! But she

didn't open the letter. She just let it sit there where Sheila had dropped it on her blanket. And she looked at it while I looked at her.

Finally she saw me staring. "What are you looking at?" she asked, frowning.

"You, silly, how come you're not opening your letter? Is it from your parents?"

"Tuffy, do you mind looking at your own mail?"

"Sure, okay, sorry."

Iris picked up her letter and went out on the porch. I opened my package. Inside was my hockey mask, my stuffed cat and a newspaper article . . . No nose plugs, Mallomars or salami. There was also a letter.

Thursday

Dear Betsy,

Here are the things you asked for. Hope it's okay.

Took Jeannie to the beach yesterday. She just loves the sand and the ocean, and screamed her head off when it was time to go home. I had to drag her off the lifeguard's stand and all the way to the parking lot. I got a terrible sunburn and cut my foot on a shell. Don't worry, it wasn't bad.

I'm enclosing an article I thought you'd enjoy about cats that was in last Sunday's *Newsday*.

I'm so glad you're at that lovely camp. It's so hot here. One of these years we're going to have to get an air conditioner. I've been spending most of the days in the supermarket and the drug store to get cool. Of course, you can't just stand around so I have to shop. I don't know where I'm going to put all the Pepto Bismol, band-aids, shaving cream, Noxema and Preparation H. We couldn't possibly use it all up. Do you think I should send some to your canteen?

Keep having a wonderful summer, darling.
Love and kisses,
Mom

I looked at the folded-up article. It was all about a new pitcher the Detroit Tigers just signed. It was a funny article but it sure wasn't about cats. I just love my mom . . . She always makes our family laugh a lot. Guess I'll have to wait to get home to see my catcher's mitt.

Iris came back in from the porch. She was smiling. I watched her put the letter in her cubby, and decided I would definitely not ask her about it or anything it said. If she wanted to talk about it, then she'd talk about it. I would learn to keep my mouth shut and mind my own business for a change . . .

But she'd never talk about it.

"Iris, what'd they say?"

"They're in Paris. At the George V."

"What's the George sank?"

"Its a hotel. It's supposed to be very beautiful. Mama said she bought me some perfume."

"Do you like French perfume?" I asked.

"Who wouldn't like French perfume!" Nat said, aiming her post card at the waste basket.

"It's all right," Iris said. "I like 'Joy' a lot, and 'Norell'."

"Oh, I *love* 'Norell'!" Nat said.

"She wears it to gym every day," I said.

Nat wrinkled her nose at me.

"Who was your card from?" Adele asked her.

"Art Maselli . . . He's a boy I met when we went to Florida last winter. He was a lifeguard on the beach."

"Why'd you throw his card away?" I wanted to know.

"Because he lives in Florida, silly. What can you do with a boy when you're in Great Neck and he's in Florida?"

Iris took out her guitar and this time she played "Be Kind to Your Parents" and we all sang until the end of Rest Hour.

Sunday

I'm not writing anymore after this because you'll be here next weekend. Don't forget to bring nose plugs.

Guess what, we won inspection! Well, we tied. This morning at Line-Up, Uncle Otto announced that our bunk and Freshman Girls Bunk Two came in first with all tens and one nine. We have to share the pennant with them. Verna was annoyed because Bunk Two is all six-year-old kids, and everybody knows their counselors do all the work for them. But at least we showed Uncle Otto we weren't all that bad. He gave the pennant to them first because they're younger. I hate cleaning.

Tonight we're having a campfire. The canteen ran out of insect repellent, so please bring some. What's Preparation H? Also, try to remember my catcher's mitt. Remember I asked you for that and you sent my hockey mask, which I can't use since there's no ice on the lake in July.

Daddy, the Gikki story you sent Iris was just terrific. It really made her happy. Thanks a lot. But yesterday she got a letter from her own parents and that was skyrockets and balloons. Thanks for writing me often.

                              Love,
                              Your daughter,
                              Tuffy

14

Ghost stories are the best part of a campfire, the scarier the better. And I never heard anyone tell them like Major Cameron. Maybe it's because he's got an English accent. Anything sounds good with an English accent. He's the Nature Counselor and I think he's kind of old to be a counselor, but it doesn't matter because he's a very gentle person and everyone likes him. Sometimes he tells stories at the end of milktime on the Quad, or if it's raining we go into the Rec Hall and he tells them there. I'm not sure what war he was in but we all call him "The Major." And he wears khaki safari clothes all the time.

He had them on when we got to the campfire site, but at night he wears long pants instead of Bermudas. We brought our extra blankets and spread them out on the grass. Verna brought a pillow. Adele and I tried to get Iris to bring her guitar, but she wouldn't. Debbie brought the candy she bought at canteen and put it all down on the blanket.

"Debbie, do you think you'll have enough to get you through the campfire?" Natalie asked when she saw the Tootsie Rolls, Milky Way, Nestle's Crunch and Milk Duds.

"Only if I don't have to share," Debbie said.

Natalie said, "I know someone who loves you, Debbie."

"Who?"

"Your dentist."

They were beginning to get the fire started. It was going to be a huge bonfire. The wood was really piled high. Gee, that looks so pretty at night. "Adele," I said, "remember the bonfire they had the last night of camp last year?"

"Yeah. It was nice. We sang 'Friends, Friends, Friends' and the whole camp cried."

"*I* didn't cry," I said. "They spoiled the mood when they sang that sticky camp alma mater."

"Oh, you mean that song they put to the tune of 'April in Paris'?" Nat asked.

"Right," I answered, " 'Summer in Skowhegan' didn't quite make it."

"I thought it was pretty," said Nat.

I looked around. Iris and Sheila had brought stationery and they were both scribbling away before it got too dark to see.

The other bunks were beginning to arrive and set down their blankets.

"Hi, Sheila."

Sheila looked up and there was Ron, the Senior Boys' counselor.

"Hi, Ron," she said.

"How about if we sit here next to your girls?"

"Sure, if you want."

Debbie and Adele made low whistling noises.

"Hey, guys," said Ron, "you put the stuff down here."

"Natalie," I whispered.

"What?"

"Don't look now, but when I tell you, look at the boy with the red and yellow rugby shirt on . . . Okay *now*."

"So?" she asked.

"Do you think he's cute?"

"He's a baby!"

"He's *not* a baby, he's fourteen."

Natalie raised an eyebrow and then she smiled, "You like him, Tuffy?"

"Shhhh! No, but he's nice. He's so dark."

"Ohhhh, Tuf-fy!" Natalie said, grinning.

"Shut up, Natalie! I'm sorry I said anything."

Uncle Otto was getting ready to start the program. The Major and Paul were lighting the torches they would use to get the bonfire going, and some of the Junior Counselors were taking out marshmallows from packages. Next to them was a big pile of green sticks we had all gathered to toast the marshmallows on.

"Good evening, Camp."

"Good *eve-ning, Un-cle Ot-to*," the camp sang back.

"Paul will begin our campfire tonight by playing a few songs for us. Bunk Twelve, will you choose the first song?" And Uncle Otto stepped back.

Bunk Twelve picked "Greensleeves", which Iris does better and I told her so. She just smiled.

After the songs, Barbara-Jean, the Arts and Crafts Counselor, did a magic act. She wasn't too bad. She pulled a quarter out of Arnold's ear, a baby bunny out of some little boy's hat and about a thousand scarves out of her jacket pocket. *Finally* it was time for stories. The Major appeared from the bushes somewhere with a tall three-legged stool, which he set up close to the fire. I don't know how he could stay that close to the heat, but it looked fantastic, almost like he was sitting in the middle of the flames with the stars in back of him. The only sounds you could hear were a cricket and a bullfrog. And then the Major started to talk.

"Once upon a time, a well-to-do businessman was about to hail a taxicab in a big city, when he was stopped by a beautiful woman dressed all in black. She didn't say a word, but handed him a calling card and disappeared into the crowd. The bewildered man looked at the card. It had some writing on it, but the alphabet was strange and he didn't even know what language it was. When he reached his destination, he asked some people he knew if they could read the writing. One man, who was Indian, said he recognized it as an ancient language. He said he would take it home that night and see if he could translate it with the aid of some of his books.

"The next morning, the Indian man returned the card. His manner was tense and angry. He said, 'I have translated the words. Never speak to me or look at me again.' And he walked away without telling the businessman what the card said.

"The businessman approached his partner and explained what had happened. The partner said, 'That certainly is strange behavior. I have a friend at an embassy. I will take the card to him and see if he will translate it for you.'

"Later in the day, the business partner returned the card to the man, saying, 'Our partnership is dissolved. I never want to see you again.'

"The man was stunned. Now he *had* to find out what the card said. He brought it home to his wife, who was devastated by his story. She would help get to the bottom of the mystery. 'I have a friend who is a fortune-teller,' said the wife. 'She is well-versed in many languages, ancient and modern. If anyone can translate the writing on this card, I'm sure she can.' And, taking the card from her husband, she left immediately for the fortune-teller's house on the outskirts of town.

" 'Yes, I can read it,' said the fortune-teller, and the wife listened.

"The man was anxiously waiting when his wife returned. But she did not speak. She handed him the card and went upstairs. Soon she came down with her suitcase and those of their children. She departed without a word.

"The poor man was, by this time, almost insane. Dazed, he left his house and began to walk the streets. As he looked up, she suddenly appeared, the beautiful woman in black who had given him the card. He began to run to catch her as she made her way through the busy crowd. She went up the stairs of a large brownstone house and disappeared into it. The man followed and began to pound on the door with its heavy brass knocker.

"The door was opened by an old lady, a servant, who refused the man's pleadings to be admitted. Her mistress was ill, perhaps dying, and had gone directly to her bedroom to rest. The man, in desperation, told her his story and begged to see the lady of the house, if only for a moment. The servant finally agreed.

"He was shown to a room at the top of a curved stairway. He knocked softly, and, when no one answered, he went in. It was very dark in the room. The heavy curtains were drawn and the lovely lady was lying on a velvet chaise. He asked if she remembered him. She did. 'Then,' he pleaded, 'you must know why it is so important for me to understand the meaning of the card.' He handed it to her. She seemed very weak, but took it and tried to read aloud. As she started to speak, she was overcome by a fit of coughing. She lay back on the chaise, gasping for air. The card fluttered from her fingers. Shaken, the man picked it up and, as she drew her last breath, watched in horror as the writing faded from the card."

Nobody moved. The Major relit his pipe and sat back on the stool.

"Well, what did it say?" Verna asked. "What did the card say?"

"You never *learn* what it says," Iris said. "That's the whole point."

"I don't get it," Adele said.

"Did you like the story?" Sheila asked.

"Yes," Adele said, "but I still want to know what the card said."

"Me, too," Verna said.

"Hey, it's time for marshmallows!" Debbie called and we all ran.

After the marshmallows, Uncle Otto told us it was time to go back to the bunks, but the whole camp set up such a roar for one more story that he finally gave in.

Puffing away on his pipe, the Major sat down again on the stool. The cheering stopped immediately and all you could hear were the crickets again. And the Major began:

"Many years ago on the island of Haiti, there lived a man and his servant. The servant was a good man and tried hard to please, but his master was cruel and often beat him. He could not leave his master, for the servant was old and would not be able to find other work. As little as he was paid, he needed the money for he had a young sister at home who could not speak and could not hear. She was afraid to leave their small hut, but spent her days keeping it clean, cooking their meager meals and waiting for her brother to return each evening.

"After many months of ill-treatment, the servant returned home one night and fell on his straw mattress. His little sister removed his shirt and found great red welts and dried blood where he had been whipped. Before her brother could stop her, she fled from the hut and, for the first time, left their little plot of land. As weak and sick as he was, her brother set out to follow her and saw she was headed for the house of his master. It took him a very long time to get there. When he arrived, the door was opened by the wicked man himself. The servant asked for his sister but was told that no one was there. 'Go away,' the man said, 'or you will be beaten again.'

'There was nothing for the servant to do but limp slowly home and wait for the morning. Upon arriving at his master's house the next day, he again asked for the girl but was ignored. Unable to endure it any longer, he began a frantic search of the house. In a tiny attic room he found her small body. She had died of fright.

"In a frenzy, the man ran from the house. He ran until he reached his cabin and, in rage and tears, he began to fashion a doll from mud clay. He worked and worked until the doll began to take on a familiar wicked expression. From his own body, he tore a shirt that had once been his master's and had been thrown out for rags. He put it on the doll's body. He then added more bits and pieces until the doll seemed the image of the evil master. When it was ready, he spoke mysterious ancient words over and over, gaining strength from the chanting. At last he pulled a pin from his ragged trousers and jabbed the doll through the heart. He dropped the doll to the floor, where it fell with one arm across its head, the other across its chest.

"The next morning the servant arrived at the master's house. Letting himself in, he saw what he had expected to find. The master was lying across the rug in his chamber, one arm clutching his chest, the other flung over his face."

"What'd you think of that last story?" Adele asked after the lights were out and Sheila had gone off with some of the other counselors.

"Oh, it was great!" Debbie said. "Did the servant kill the master through the doll, or what?"

"How could you say it was great if you don't know that?" I asked. "Sure, the doll was supposed to be the symbol of the master. That's why he made it look like him."

"It was a voodoo doll."

"A what?" Nat asked.

"A voodoo doll," Iris repeated. "It's a kind of magic they do on small islands like Haiti, and also in Africa and other parts of the world."

"Voodoo magic?" I asked.

"Voodoo, right. It's one of the black arts and it's used a lot for revenge. If you want to get someone, the quickest way is through voodoo."

"Is that in those books you read, Iris?" asked Adele.

"A lot of it is. Magical cults are very interesting, *I* think, anyway," she added.

15

Wednesday was Sheila's day off. She was really excited, and so were we, because this was the day she was hitching to meet Bob in Narrowsburg.

"Come on, girls, would you get this bunk in shape?" Debbie said. "Sheila can't leave until Clean-Up is over."

"Yes, *please*," Sheila said, "I need all the time I can get if I'm going to get there and back by curfew."

"It's only eight-*thirty*," Verna said. "You'll have fifteen-and-a-half *hours!*"

"But it'll take hours to get there, especially hitching," Adele said, "and she wants to spend some *time* with the guy, after all!"

Natalie won Miss Clean-Up that day. Anything to do with "true love" was worth working for, so she was the one who made sure all the jobs were done. Verna asked Uncle Otto to inspect our bunk first.

Sheila was dressed in her "city clothes", which means a dress, when Uncle Otto came to inspect. No one wears a dress unless it's her day off. I mean, who's going to wear a dress to volleyball? "Day off, Sheila?" Uncle Otto asked, trying to bounce a coin on Debbie's bed. It just lay there.

"Yes, Uncle Otto."

"Want a lift into Honesdale?"

"Oh yes, thank you. That would be great!" Sheila started to reach for her things.

"Louise will be driving the van into town in about an hour," he said, as he tucked in a shirttail on a shelf in my cubby.

"Sheila's face fell. "Oh, well, then, uh, I guess I'll skip it. I'm in kind of a hurry."

"So was your bunk. You should have taken a little more time with your clean-up. The beds are loose, the cubbies untidy and there's a bathing suit hanging over the porch railing. You get a six."

"Why a six?" Verna asked after he'd gone, "he only named three things wrong."

"Maybe two beds were loose," Nat said. "Anyway, I hate my bed that tight. When he can bounce a coin off it, you can never get into it at night. You have to *pry* the blankets out of the mattress."

"Yeah," I said, "but if you sneak down into the covers without moving them, and you lie in one position all night without turning over, then you don't have to make the bed again in the morning."

"You also have to weigh twenty pounds, and be

drugged when you go to sleep so you don't move," Debbie said.

"No, you can hypnotize yourself not to move in your sleep," Iris said. Everyone stopped talking because usually Iris didn't join in our conversations too much . . . especially when we were hacking around.

Sheila asked, "What do you mean 'hypnotize yourself'?"

"Well," Iris explained, "if you talk to yourself at night right before the moment you fall asleep, you can sometimes tell yourself what to dream, or how to feel when you wake up, or anything you want. And it'll work because your mind is very open at that time and your subconscious is right on the surface. I read that in a book."

"What do you mean 'your subconscious is right on the surface'?" Nat asked.

"That means that you are at a point right between dreaming and being awake. It's kind of like a never-never-land, like limbo. If you have a strong enough will, you can master your mind for the rest of the night. The trick is to catch it at that exact moment when you are so drowsy you can hardly stand to be awake, and then you wish for something very hard."

The bunk got very quiet while Iris was talking. Everyone had walked over to sit on her bed. I don't know if they believed what she was saying, but I knew we were all going to try to "catch" our minds that night.

Sheila jumped up suddenly, "I've got to go! Anyone want me to bring anything back?"

"Hens' teeth," said Natalie.

"Oh, Nat," Sheila said.

"Well, how much room could they take up?" Nat said.

" 'Bye, Sheila," we all yelled, "have a wonderful day!" She turned and waved to us as we all went out on the porch to watch her walk to the main road.

"Who's our counselor today?" asked Adele.

"I think Marcia," Deb said.

"Every time I see Marcia I think of that night," said Natalie, "when Uncle Otto made her babysit for me."

"Well, her job didn't last long. We were all back at the bunk ten minutes later," I said. "Anyway, Marcia's all right. Hey, anyone want to play jacks?"

"We can't," Verna said, "we've got to go to First Activity."

"We can play until the bugle blows," Debbie said, and went inside to get the jacks.

"I don't want to play. I just feel like reading," Iris said, and she sat on Trunk Number Two with one of her big books.

We went around the circle to see who would go first. Adele won by picking up the most jacks. On her first turn a jack dropped through a hole in the porch floor. "Rats!" Adele said.

"Rats? Not yet, you haven't even finished threesies," I said.

"Go get the jack, Adele," Debbie said.

"I don't wanna go under there," Adele said.

"Well, you dropped it," Debbie insisted. "Come on, they're my jacks."

Adele walked down the steps and peered under the porch. "I don't see it."

"Of course not, dummy, you have to get under there," Nat said. "I'll put something through the hole so you can see where you dropped it." Without getting up, she began to look around the porch for something to put down the hole.

"Oh, all right," Adele muttered and began to crawl under. "It's damp and crummy down here," she complained. "And I can't see what you put in the hole."

"That's because I haven't put anything in there yet. There's nothing on the porch. I'll just put my finger through," Nat yelled. "See it?"

"No."

"Oh, jeez, my finger's stuck!"

"I don't see your finger, Nat!" Adele yelled.

"I don't see it *either*, dammit!" Natalie screeched.

"Natalie, don't *pull* it," offered Verna.

"Well if I don't pull it, it won't come *out!*"

"Oh, gosh, don't get upset," Verna said, getting upset.

Suddenly there was a scream from under the porch and Adele came shooting out.

"What's wrong with *you?*" Debbie wanted to know.

"There was a big *spider!*" Adele wailed, teary-eyed and shuddering.

Iris put down her book and came over to the steps.

"Oh, for Pete's sake, Adele," Debbie said.

"What'd it look like?" Iris asked.

"It was *hairy!*" Adele sobbed. "It crawled on my *hand!*"

"Is *somebody* going to do *something* about my finger?" Natalie screamed.

"Did you get my jack?" Debbie asked.

"Did you get the spider?" asked Iris.

"I've got an idea, Nat," Verna said, going to the door. "Soapy water will loosen your finger!" And she disappeared inside.

"Soap is her answer to *everything!*" Natalie hollered, clutching her wrist.

"You know, a spider may not be *just* a spider," Iris said, half to herself.

"What does *that* mean?" Debbie asked.

"Well, I was just reading about spiders and witchcraft—"

"Oh, for Lord's sake!" Natalie cried.

"What, Iris, what?" I wanted to know.

Verna came out with a cookie tin filled with soapy water which she began to pour on Nat's finger. "Wiggle it," she told Nat.

"What about spiders and witchcraft? What?" I tugged at Iris's arm.

Iris went on, "A witch usually has an animal with her at all times. Sometimes it's a black cat . . . Sometimes it's a big hairy spider. But they're not really animals, they're guiding spirits for the witches. They call them 'familiars'."

"My finger's still stuck, Verna!"

"Wiggle it more," Verna said.

"Ohhhhhh!" Nat sighed with relief as her finger finally slid out of the hole. "Thanks, Verna," she mumbled as she sucked on her finger, which was all blue and puffy.

"Go put it under cold water for a minute," Verna said.

As soon as Nat's finger was freed, Iris was off and under the porch like a shot.

"Where are you going?" Adele asked.

"You shouldn't have been so upset, Adele," came Iris's muffled voice. "That spider may have been your 'familiar'. Think of it . . . Your own personal guiding spirit."

Just then the bugle blew.

"Iris, come on out of there," Adele called, sounding nervous.

"Coming." We were all peering over the edge of the porch as Iris's head appeared. She was moving along on her stomach because her hands were cupped together. Adele screamed and jumped back, but Iris stood up and began to mount the steps, still cupping her hands.

"Don't come near me!" Adele shrieked as she and Verna started to back toward the wall.

Iris slowly began to open her hands and, as everybody's eyes widened in horror, she smiled a kind of weird smile I'd never seen before. Then she shoved her left hand in our faces and revealed Debbie's jack.

16

"'Morning, girls," Marcia sang cheerfully, as she approached our bunk. Then she frowned, "What's the matter with you?"

"They were expecting a guiding spirit," Iris said. "I couldn't find it."

"Huh?" Marcia said.

"Nothing," Debbie giggled.

"Well, let's get a move-on," Marcia said, back in her cheery mood. "We're going to be late for badminton and volleyball."

Marcia was with us for the whole day. Every bunk has a junior counselor on the regular counselor's day off but this was the first time we'd had Marcia. She was nice but she reminded me of the kind of Girl Scout leader who wears her uniform to all the meetings, even on crummy days. With Marcia, we got to every activity on time, to every meal on time. Nobody got in trouble, but nobody laughed too much either. Natalie didn't go looking for Paul the whole day. I guess we were all think-ing of Sheila, hoping she was able to get to Nar-rowsburg, and that Bob was too.

Anyway, I was anxious for Lights-Out that night. I wanted to see if I could "catch" my mind at the moment before going to sleep. I decided two things . . . That I wouldn't move in the bed all night, and that I would dream about being a fa-mous movie star like Tatum O'Neal.

Finally we finished the evening activity which was a treasure hunt, girls' camp against the boys', and the girls lost. The treasure turned out to be a watermelon, which I hate anyway. We got back to our bunk early. "Who's the O.D. tonight?" I asked. O.D. stands for "On Duty", the counselors who walk around the camp at night and make sure everything's okay, and nobody's sick or sneaking out. There are usually four O.D. counselors, two for the girls' camp and two for the boys'. The other counselors are off, and they're allowed to go into town if they want. But at the midnight curfew, they all have to be back at their bunks.

"I'm O.D. tonight," Marcia said, "and I'd really better get started on the rounds now. Will you girls turn out your own light when the bugle blows Taps?"

We said we would and, as soon as she left, I jumped up on my bed. "Well?" I asked.

"Well, what?" said Debbie. She was putting on her "bunny" pajamas which came with a nightcap that had ears. It got us hysterical the first few times she wore it, especially after the camp laundry lost the wires for the ears and they came back limp and hanging like two old socks.

"Well, are we going to try to 'catch' our minds tonight and plan our dreams?"

Iris looked up.

"*I'm* going to do it," Nat said, "and I'm going to dream that Paul sings all his songs only to me."

"What a surprise!" I said.

"I'm going to dream I'm elected president of my class in the fall," said Adele, "and the first thing I'm going to do is give the whole school Fridays off."

"You can't do that," said Verna.

"It's *my* dream," Adele insisted, "maybe I'll throw in Thursdays, too."

"What are you going to dream, Verna?" asked Nat.

"I don't believe you can decide what you're going to dream," Verna answered.

"But aren't you even going to try it?" I wanted to know.

"Have *you* done it, Iris?" Verna asked.

"I've tried it," Iris answered.

"And?"

"And I never remember my dreams in the morning, so I don't know if it worked."

"Try it tonight," I said. "Let's all try it and see if any of us can do it, okay?"

Taps blew just then, and Verna pulled the light cord.

"Okay, ready?" I asked.

"No, I'm not tired," said Nat. "What do you think Sheila's doing?"

"Well, it's after nine, so she ought to be trying to hitch home. Otherwise she'll never make it," Verna answered.

"I'm going to dream that I got locked in Baskin-Robbins all night long, and made and ate every single sundae on their list," Debbie said.

"And you'd have to spend the rest of your life there," Adele said, "because they wouldn't be able to get you out the door."

"I wouldn't care," Deb said.

"You'd split your bunny pajamas," I said. We all started to laugh, picturing Debbie in her split bunny pajamas with her limp ears hanging down over her round cheeks.

"Iris, are you going to try it?" I asked.

"I don't know, maybe," she answered drowsily. Through the curtain on the screen door, I could see the O.D.s' flashlights waving around the Quad. They shined for a minute into our bunk but no one came in. I closed my eyes and started to think very hard about the speech I would make when I won the Academy Award. But I wasn't at all sleepy. Everyone was quiet.

"Natalie, are you up?"

"No."

"Okay, okay . . ."

I tried to concentrate again but it was no use. I was wide awake. I decided to go out on the porch because that always helps me get my thoughts together. I slipped out quietly but, as I was sitting down on the first step, a flashlight shined in my face.

"Who *is* that?" someone hissed at me.

"Me, Tuffy. Who's that?"

"Marcia and Ruthie. Get back inside, Tuffy, and go to sleep."

"I can't sleep. That's why I'm outside," I answered.

"You're in trouble if you don't move it, Tuffy."

"Oh, boy!" I went back in but it was hot and I knew I wouldn't fall asleep ... just when I wanted to so badly. I got a comic book and flashlight out of my cubby, lay down and began to read.

I woke up when I accidently rolled over on my flashlight, which was still turned on. Everything was dark and quiet. Darn, I never got to "catch" my mind. I could see Verna's little alarm clock on the floor facing me. Oh! Wow! Twelve-fifteen! I sat up and looked at Sheila's bed. It was empty.

"Hey!" I said softly. "Hey, get up! Come on, wake up!"

"Mmmmmmm," Adele said.

"*Get up!*"

"Tuffy, are you crazy?" Natalie asked. "What's wrong with you?"

"Sheila's not back yet."

"So?"

"So it's twelve-fifteen. She missed curfew. What'll we do?"

"What *can* we do?"

"I don't know," I said, "think of something."

"Make a big life-size doll of her to fool everybody ... A great big voodoo doll. G'night," and Natalie turned over.

"Natalie, wait, that gives me an idea. Let's stuff her bed."

"Wha?"

"Get some extra blankets and put them in her bed, so if Uncle Otto comes in he'll think she's sleeping."

"That's no good, Tuffy. She has to sign in at the H.C. shack when she comes in. He'll know she's not back."

"But, if she doesn't sign in, maybe he'll think she forgot and come here to see."

"Okay." Natalie got out of bed and so did Adele; the others were still sleeping. We got together some blankets and sheets and arranged them in Sheila's bed. Just as we finished, we could see a flashlight swinging outside our window. And the light in the H.C. shack was still on.

We leaped back into our beds as the door creaked open and the curtain was pushed aside. It was Uncle Otto. Nobody could miss him, even in the dark. His flashlight passed over all our faces and stopped at Sheila's bed. I opened one eye but he wasn't looking at me. He bent down and began to poke at the form in the bed. Some nerve, I thought. Suddenly he peeled off the blanket and saw what was really there. He just stood for a long time.

Then: "Tuffy, I know you're up." Very quietly.

"Yeah."

"You stuffed the bed to protect your counselor?"

"Yeah."

He looked at me, shining his flashlight right in my face. "Did you ever consider," he began slowly, "that perhaps she's been hurt, or had an accident?

And that someone of responsibility ought to know about it and be ready in case he's needed?"

"No," I answered.

He turned and walked quickly out of the bunk. "I wonder how he knew it was me."

"What a surprise," Natalie said.

I must have dozed off again because the next thing I heard was the creak of the screen door. I never heard it before at night, but I guess I wasn't sleeping very soundly. I was wide awake as soon as I realized that it was Sheila. She closed the door softly and sat down on her bed. It was getting light. The sun would be up soon.

"Sheila? What time is it?"

"Quarter of five."

"Oh, Sheila!"

She put her head in her hands.

"*Sheila?* What happened?"

"I got fired," she answered.

17

I don't remember sleeping during the rest of the night at all, but I must have because when Verna's alarm went off I opened my eyes and was surprised to find it was morning. Uncle Otto had already done his wake-up yelling . . . The alarm always went off a little later and we seldom heard him anymore. Sheila was still wearing her dress from the day before and she was closing a suitcase on her bed. I felt sick.

Verna leaped out of bed like she always does (how can she *do* that?) and turned off the alarm.

"What's going on? What are you doing, Sheila?" she asked.

"What does it look like she's doing?" I yelled at her. "She's *packing!* She got *fired!*"

All the eyes opened at that. All the mouths started flapping. Sheila closed the suitcase and started filling up another one. But she couldn't do much because, by now, all the girls were on her bed, all talking at once and sitting on her clothes. She gave up and just sat down and cried. Well, you can't answer questions when you're crying, so everyone just shut up and sat there too. Somebody handed her some tissues and finally she quieted down and told us her story.

"I got in at four-fifteen this morning. As I walked up the road I could see him just sitting on the steps of the H.C. shack looking at me. I started apologizing and telling him what happened, but you know how he is. He never said *anything*. He just got up when I was through and said, 'Pack up and be out of here by the time breakfast is over!' and he walked away."

"I *hate* him!" I said.

"Without even listening! What a rat!" Nat said.

"What did happen, Sheila?" Adele finally asked. "Were you just having a really good time?"

"I *had* a good time, but that's not why I was late. I left Narrowsburg in plenty of time to get here."

"Uh oh, you got a bad hitch?" from Debbie.

"No, I'm careful which cars I get in. That wasn't it. I met Bob in front of Peter's Gate, the only nice restaurant in town. And oh, it was fantastic to see him! We had practically the whole day. We got some sandwiches from this little deli, and we had lunch in a park by a brook. Hardly anyone was around and it was so nice."

"Did you make out?" Nat, of course.

"None of your business, Natalie," I said. "Go on, Sheila."

"Well, about five o'clock I started to feel kind of

sick to my stomach, but I didn't want to tell Bob and ruin the whole day. So I kept quiet and thought if I just tried to forget it, it would go away."

"But it didn't?"

"It didn't. It got worse. I finally had to tell him I wasn't feeling too well and he wanted to come back here with me, but that would have been dumb. He never would have gotten back to Ellenville in time to work his shift. It's hard to get a hitch at four o'clock in the morning."

Iris said, "Why didn't you just call up the camp and say you were sick and stuck in another town? That way, Uncle Otto would have been prepared."

"I don't know why I didn't do that," Sheila answered. "I didn't think I was that sick. I thought I could make it back. It was only about seven-thirty and I had 'til midnight. But it kept getting worse and worse. I got a ride with a lady and her little boy and that was lucky because she turned out to be a nurse. She said it was probably food poisoning, you know, from those deli sandwiches."

"Well, didn't Bob get it, too?" Adele asked.

"No, we figured out it was the mayonnaise. He didn't have a sandwich with mayo. That spoils so easily in the summer. This lady, Mrs. Mackenzie, said that was probably it. Anyway, she took me right to a hospital. They gave me lots of water and made me throw up, which I did for about a thousand hours. Then I got so exhausted I fell asleep. I had to take a *cab* back here. It cost me twenty dollars!" She started to cry again.

"Uncle Otto probably didn't believe you," Verna said. "He probably thought you were making it up."

"Even if you *had* called," Nat said, "he wouldn't have believed you. He doesn't care about anybody as long as his camp runs on schedule!"

"He sounded worried last night when he found the stuffed bed," I said. "He said we shouldn't have tried to cover for you in case something was really wrong. But something *was* wrong and he didn't even believe it. As long as you're all right now, it's okay to fire you! Boy!"

"Oh, gee, they're playing Line-Up," Debbie said. But we all just sat there.

"Forget Line-Up," I said, "I'm not going. But, when it's over, I'm gonna see Uncle Otto. We *all* are!" I started to dress.

"No, Tuf," Sheila said, "don't do that. It won't do any good and you'll just get yourselves in trouble."

"But it worked before when we all stuck together about 'Mighty Joe Young'."

"It won't work, believe me," Sheila insisted. "He was taken by surprise then, but he knows us now. And it'll just make him madder. Then, when I'm gone, he'll take it out on you. Or even if he doesn't do that, it won't make him happier about this bunk. And you still have a whole month of camp to go."

"If you think we're going to sit still and just let you leave without doing anything, you're crazy! It wasn't fair, what he did!"

"Let it go, Tuffy, we're not going to change him. I mean it."

"He won't change his mind, Tuffy." It was Iris. "And certainly not for us."

"But it's not fair!"

Debbie cried, "Listen!"

"What?"

"It's Flag-Raising . . . The record's playing Flag-Raising."

"So what?"

"So our bunk's not out there. And he didn't come in after us."

"I guess he's going to leave us alone this morning," Sheila said, getting up and pulling a sweater out from under Natalie. "But don't expect it again, little girls. Not for the whole rest of the summer."

From the window we watched the rest of the camp file into the Mess Hall for breakfast. Uncle Otto was standing next to the flagpole and, as the last of the campers closed the Mess Hall doors, he turned and started toward our bunk. Verna and I were dressed, but the rest of the bunk was still in p.j.s. All of us jumped onto our beds.

He knocked twice on the screen door. Nobody said, "Come in", but he did anyway.

"Bunk Ten, you'd better finish getting dressed and go to breakfast."

I said, "We don't want any breakfast."

He said, "Tuffy, I won't have any lip from you. You all get dressed and get in there in five minutes." Door opened . . . Door closed.

We got in there in five minutes.

Marcia was at our table eating pancakes when we arrived. "Hi," she said. "Guess I'm going to be your permanent counselor from now on." No one looked at her; no one spoke; no one ate. When the camp began to leave, we all got up and went back to the bunk. Marcia didn't come with us. I guess she went back to her own bunk to pack her stuff to move to *our* bunk. Sheila was all ready to go.

"I just waited for you to say 'goodbye'," she said. "I really have to get out of here. Gee, I haven't even called my parents. Oh, Natalie!"

"What?"

"I'm sorry. I never got the hens' teeth," she sobbed. We all cried and hugged her. Her trunk and suitcases were tagged and ready to be shipped, so all she had to carry was an overnight bag. Aunt Louise was parked on the road in the van, waiting to take her into Honesdale to catch a bus. We were all crying as we watched the van pull away. It didn't help to see Marcia carrying a load of stuff into our bunk as we came back.

"Clean-Up time, girls," Marcia was saying. "Your chart says you've got Arts and Crafts for First Activity, and there isn't much time. I'll try not to get in your way." She put a bunch of towels into Sheila's cubby.

I looked at the bed we had stuffed with blankets the night before. It was stripped, just a lumpy mattress. Sheila in the bed—! blankets in the bed—! a life-size voodoo doll—!

"IRIS!" I yelled.

"What?"

"Come on outside."

"Why?"

"Come *on!*"

"Tuffy, where are you going?" Marcia asked.

"We're going to get a new broom. Ours is losing straw," I answered.

"Okay."

When we were outside I pulled Iris off the porch. "I want to make a voodoo doll," I whispered.

"*What?*"

"I want to make a voodoo doll of Uncle Otto. He deserves it and I want to do it. Do you know how?"

"Forget it."

"No, Iris, *please!* You've got all those books. You know how to do it," I begged.

"Tuffy, I never made a voodoo doll."

"Come on, Iris. We've got Arts and Crafts right after Clean-Up. We can get all the stuff we need. The other girls'll help. What do we need?"

"I don't want to start this. It's crazy," Iris insisted, and started back to the bunk.

"No, wait," I said, "just tell me what we need." She stopped walking. "You're the only one who knows all about it, Iris. I just want you to tell me how to make it."

"That's all you want to know?"

"Yeah."

"All right," she said. I pulled her closer to the Rec Hall so Marcia couldn't see us if she looked outside. "Well," she began, "you need some clay, and cloth, and you need some very personal stuff of, uh, the victim."

"What do you mean 'very personal'?"

"Well, like some of his hair and, um, fingernail cuttings."

"Fingernails?"

"Uh huh, fingernail cuttings are supposed to be very effective."

"Well, how do we get *that*?"

"Tuffy, this is *your* idea."

"I know, I know, and I'm gonna do it, too." I meant it. "Come on, let's go back in."

"Where's the broom?" Marcia asked.

"What broom?"

Marcia put her hands on her hips. "The broom you went to get because ours was losing straw."

"Oh, *that* broom! They're gonna order one for us. They didn't have any."

"Hmmm," she said. "Well, I have to get some more of my stuff. Finish your clean-up, girls!" And she was gone.

"Listen, everybody—Verna, will you quit cleaning a minute?"

They stopped and looked at me. "Today in Arts and Crafts we're going to make a voodoo doll of Uncle Otto, just like in the Major's story. We're going to get back at him for Sheila. Only don't tell *anyone* . . . Just the six of us will know."

"You're nuts, Tuf," Nat said, "that stuff is a waste of time. I didn't dream about Paul at all last night."

"Natalie, you probably didn't do it right. You probably missed the right time to "catch" your mind. I know I did. Anyway, this is worth trying. If we could talk to him, I'd say let's do that, but we can't. Now we have to get some very personal stuff of his to make the doll and you're going to help me do it."

Debbie asked, "How?"

"Iris told me what we need. We can get most of the stuff in Arts and Crafts. The other stuff will be harder. I'll get to that in a minute." I was beginning to feel a little better. There was something I could do, after all, and I was getting ideas as I went along. "First, we watch Uncle Otto when inspection starts. As soon as he goes into Bunk Eleven, Iris and I will leave and go over to his cabin."

"Ohhhhh, no!" Iris cried.

"Iris, Sheila was our counselor, so we're all in this together."

"Tuffy, you said all you wanted was for me to tell you what you needed."

"But, Iris, you *said* you had never done this before. Aren't you curious? And, besides, you know he deserves it. Sheila lost her job! For Pete's sake, don't you care?"

Iris was quiet.

"Besides, I *said* I was willing to talk to him and *you* were the one who said he'd never listen. Are we just gonna let him get away with it?"

All the girls were paying attention now, so I went on. "Aunt Louise will probably be at the infirmary for the morning sick-call and nobody will be at their cabin. Then, Iris, you stand guard outside and I'll go in and take what we need for the doll."

"What if someone comes?" Iris said. "I don't like this."

"We'll have a signal," I said as the thought came to me. "Can you make an animal sound?"

"An animal sound?"

"Yeah, so it'll sound natural."

"Maybe she can moo," Debbie offered.

"Moo?" Nat said. "When was the last time you saw a cow hanging around camp?"

"Well, Tuffy said 'animal sound'." Debbie sounded hurt.

"I can croak," Iris said.

"Let's hear."

"Ribbit," Iris said.

"Deeper," said Adele.

"*Ribbit.*"

"Get the sound in back of your throat more," Nat said. "Put your hand on your Adam's Apple like this.

"Like this?" Iris asked. "*Rib-bit!*"

"A frog in pain," Nat said.

"A frog in pain is good enough," I said. "Now, while we're gone, you four stall him in here as long as you can. Point out all the terrific little jobs you did cleaning up."

"Tuffy, you're supposed to be here for inspection. What if he asks where you girls are? What do we tell him?" Verna asked.

"Tell him we're at the infirmary. I really am feeling rotten anyway," I answered. "Okay?"

Blank looks.

"OKAY?" I shouted.

"Yeah," Adele said. "Go ahead."

"Okay," Iris said, nodding slowly.

"Hey! I didn't have any breakfast," Debbie said.

We laughed for the first time since *forever*. It felt good. Then we went into a frenzy of a clean-up.

18

When Iris and I reached Uncle Otto's cabin, we crouched down behind some big pricker bushes that hid his tiny yard.

"Can you see anything through the bushes?" I whispered to Iris.

She peered through. "No," she whispered back, "the bushes are too thick."

"I'll see if I can part them. *Ow!*"

"Shhh!"

"Sorry. Listen, I'm going to peek around them. Stay back." I scrunched down on my stomach and crawled to the edge of a bush. The cabin door was wide open and Aunt Louise was outside on her knees in front of a little vegetable garden. I backed toward Iris, still on my stomach. "She's weeding her garden," I said.

"Well, then let's go back. Come on," Iris said.

"No, wait. She's got to go to the infirmary some time. She's late now. Let's just stay another minute."

Iris looked around. "What if somebody comes? We look silly just sitting here behind these bushes."

"Well, let's think of something we can be doing so we don't look silly," I suggested.

"I can't think of anything that would sound like a good reason for our being here at all."

She was right, but I was determined to get in there. "Look, no one's coming. Just a little while more, please, Iris."

"Okay." We sat back and picked at the grass.

"I miss Sheila," I said.

"I do, too," Iris said, nodding.

"That's why I really want to do this thing . . . make the voodoo doll. He's been rotten to us ever since the first day." I was getting angry all over again. "Does the doll have to look *exactly* like him?"

"As much as possible," Iris answered. "The main thing is, the doll has to wear things of his that are very close to his body. That's why hair and finger-nails or toenails are good things. Then it's like he and the doll are one."

"So the more things you use of his very own, the better, right?"

"Did you want something, girls?" There stood Aunt Louise.

We had forgotten to whisper.

Both of us jumped to our feet. "Hi, Aunt Louise," I began. "No, uh, we were just—I mean, we thought—Gee, that's a nice cucumber you've got there."

"It's a zucchini," said Aunt Louise.

Just then the bugle blew First Activity.

"Oh. Wow! There's the bugle; we'd better go." Iris and I started to move. "Thanks a lot, Aunt Louise," I called over my shoulder.

"You're welcome," I heard as we ran toward the Quad.

We met the bunk on the way to Archery.

"What happened?" Debbie hissed.

"Did you get anything?" Nat asked.

"Did you get caught?" Adele wanted to know.

"Aunt Louise was there so we couldn't get in," I answered. "But we'll use the same plan for tomorrow morning . . . Fast clean-up and stalled inspection. I'm sure it'll be better then because it's Friday, the day before Parents' Weekend, and Uncle Otto and Aunt Louise will have a lot to do. They won't be hanging around their cabin. Okay?" Everyone nodded. "Okay, Iris?"

"Yes," she answered. "I said I would."

That afternoon at Rest Hour, I got a letter from Daddy.

Tuesday

Dear Bets,

Can't wait to see you on Saturday. We should be arriving around one-thirty or two. It's really been lonely around here without our big girl.

Jeannie has learned the word 'bathroom' and likes to yell it a lot. Her favorite places for yelling 'bathroom' are the supermarket on Saturday morning; between stops on the subway in New York City; the public library; and after she's gone to bed. Your mom knows the location of every bathroom on the east coast.

Your letters sound like you're having a fine time and I'm glad that you seem so fond of the girls in your bunk. We're looking forward to meeting all of them. And that reminds me— Please be sure and ask your friend, Iris, to come out for dinner with us on Saturday night. Of course, we were planning to take you and we'd like to have her join us. Glad she enjoyed Gikki. Don't tell her who does his typing.

Love,
Dad

Oh, Daddy, what a great idea! I put down the letter. Iris was outside on the porch getting a bathing suit that had dried on the railing, so I went out there.

"Iris, I have an invitation for you," I said, closing the screen door behind me.

"What?"

"We want you to come out for dinner with us on Saturday night, okay?"

She looked up, frowning, "You mean with your parents? They don't even know me."

"They know you're my friend," I said, "and I have it in writing that my father wants you to come."

"Listen, Tuffy, you don't have to do that. You

haven't seen your parents all month. You probably have things you want to talk over with them."

"Yeah, well, they don't have to be all talked over on Saturday night. I really want you to come, Iris. I should have thought of it myself. It was my father's idea."

"Really?"

"Really! He's a nice man. You'll like him . . . Mom, too."

"Thanks, Tuffy, that'd be nice," she said, almost whispering. Then, cheerily, "I mean, I know my parents want me to have dinner with *them*, only I don't have the right clothes for Maxim's!"

"What's Maxim's?"

"A restaurant in Paris."

"Oh."

"It's okay, Tuffy. I'm used to it. Really. I've been through Parents' Weekends before. They're just like any other weekend."

"Sure," I said, "but this one won't be. You'll be with us."

19

The next morning we were all set again. Iris and I left the bunk separately. Iris told Marcia that she had to go to the infirmary for cough medicine, and I said I had to go to the Mess Hall to get a sweater I'd left there.

This time, there was no one at Uncle Otto's cabin. Iris had checked out the infirmary and Aunt Louise was there. The cabin door was closed, but I knew it wouldn't be locked. No one ever locks anything in camp. "Remember the signal," I reminded Iris, "the frog's croak. But do it so I can hear it." She nodded and went around to the back of the cabin, where there were some thick trees.

I knocked softly on the door, just to make absolutely sure there was no one inside. There was no answer, so I went in, closing the door behind me.

It was only one room; the walls were logs and there was a big fireplace on one side. I bet they really use that fireplace on some of the nights up here. On the wall opposite the fireplace there was a large double bed with a patchwork quilt on it, and there was a braided rug on the wooden floor. It was a pretty room; I really liked it. What I wanted to do was sit on the floor in front of the fireplace, but what I had to do was get some stuff of Uncle Otto's and get out of there.

I looked on the floor next to the bed for fingernail cuttings. But then I realized that, even if I found some, how would I know they were *his* and not *hers?* I decided to forget the fingernails. The thing to do was get a piece of his clothing . . . Something he wears a lot.

One of his Ma-Sha-Na tee-shirts was thrown over a rocking chair in the corner. It was pretty soggy-looking, like he'd worn it. I picked it up. Whew! He'd definitely worn it and it hadn't been washed. Good! Now what else would be really personal?

On a little dresser next to the bed was a comb and brush set, and it wasn't a woman's. The brush was heavy tortoise shell and square-backed. I didn't see Aunt Louise's brush and comb set, but I was sure this wasn't it. I pulled out a bunch of hairs from the brush and put them in a tissue in my pocket. Just as I was looking around for some more I heard a frog croak. I felt my heart drop into my stomach. It had to be Iris. Real frogs don't gasp when they croak.

If someone was coming in, there was no way I could get out because there was only one door. I made a dive for under the bed just as the door opened. Oh, jeez, it was Uncle Otto! I could see his

feet in huge brown moccasins with blue socks. My
heart was beating so loud I was sure he could hear
it. And was I sweating! Boy, this was worse than
playing tennis! I wiped my face with his smelly
tee-shirt and prayed that he only came here to get
something and would leave right away. *What was
he doing?* He was just standing in one place, not
moving. Can you sleep standing up? Probably *he*
could. Finally he turned and walked (Oh, Lord!)
toward the *bed. Don'tsitonthebed! Ohpleasedon't-
sitonthebed!* I saw the feet turn, and I flattened
myself on the floor just in time. His weight came
down on the bed and practically *through* it. There
was a big bulge exactly one inch from my left knee.
He had to be sitting down. Oh, God, if he catches
me, please don't let him hit me. If he *doesn't* catch
me, I promise I won't lie about being allergic to
eggs and I'll be better with Jeannie and I'll do all
my homework before I go out to play. If he doesn't
catch me, I'll never complain about First-Activity
swim again and I won't ever—

The lump was lifting. The moccasins were moving. There they were, walking away from the bed
toward the door. The door was opening . . . It was
closing. I breathed for the first time in what seemed
like days, and just lay there sweating.

"Tuffy!"

The hoarse sound came from the back wall of
the cabin. I crawled out from under the bed and
whispered to the back wall, "Is he gone?" All I
wanted was *out* of that room.

"Yes."

Up and out . . . I raced for the back of the cabin where Iris looked as sick as I felt.

"He didn't *see* you in there? Where *were* you?"

"Under the bed, and I don't want to talk about it ever again."

"Did you get anything?"

"How's hairs from his brush and a dirty tee-shirt?"

"Terrific! What about fingernails?"

"No fingernails."

"Okay," she said. "Let's go."

Things really seemed to be working out. Usually we don't have Arts and Crafts two days in a row, but Uncle Otto made sure every group had it today so we could finish all our projects before Parents' Weekend. All of us except Debbie had finished projects, so we helped Debbie finish hers, two lanyards and a painted box made out of ice-cream sticks. An artist she'd never be, but she sure played a mean game of tennis.

When we finished, I told Barbara-Jean we had a bunk project we wanted to work on, so could she please leave us alone for the rest of the period. "Well, isn't there something I can help you with?" she asked. "That's what I'm here for."

I figured she was afraid we'd wreck something. "We could use a needle and thread and some clay, not the hardening kind." She looked a little funny.

"We're going to make, uh, sand candles," Adele said. "We need wax and, uh, food coloring."

"Wax! Yes, wax!" Iris said. "Perfect!"

"Oh, sand candles are fun!" said Barbara-Jean. "Let me help you."

"No! no!" Nat said. "We really want to do this by ourselves. The shapes we want to make are, uh, kind of personal. It's like a private game."

"Honest, we won't mess anything up," Debbie said.

"Well, okay," Barbara-Jean finally said. "You want me to sit outside?"

"Sure, take the activity off," I said. "Go on outside and talk to Marcia. This is only her second day of being our counselor. You could probably cheer her up."

Barbara-Jean got us a whole lot of stuff and went out to sit with Marcia. We sat down at the tables and started to sort everything. There was candle wax, about a pound of it; thick, white thread and a needle; brown soft clay wrapped in waxed paper; three bottles of vegetable coloring in blue, red and yellow; and some yarn.

"We'll use the wax instead of the clay," Iris said. "Wax is much better. Do we have anything to melt it?"

"Look around for matches," said Nat.

"No," I said, "forget melting it. We can't do that in here. We'll make the mold out of the clay and melt the wax around it later. Meanwhile, who can sew?"

"I can," Verna said.

"Okay, Verna, take this tee-shirt and rip it up. You have to make a little tee-shirt out of it to fit a doll."

"How big a doll?"

"How big, Iris?"

"I don't know. Any size. How about as big as Barbie?"

"A Barbie Doll?"

"Well, maybe a little bigger."

"A little bigger than Barbie, Verna. And be sure you use the part of the tee-shirt that has Camp Ma-Sha-Na on it. Get some of those letters on the shirt, even if you have only two or three. Adele, get some plastic strips and make a tiny lanyard out of them, like he wears around his neck with the whistle on it. It's all black."

"What about socks and shoes?" Debbie asked.

"Make the shoes out of the brown clay. He wears moccasins, brown ones. And make a pair of socks out of the leftover tee-shirt and dye them blue with the food coloring."

"Does he wear blue socks?" Nat asked me.

"He sure does."

By the time Arts and Crafts was over, we had the start of a tee-shirt, two little blue socks, a pair of clay moccasins, and part of a lanyard. The body of the doll would come later. We put all the stuff into a bag with the tissue-wrapped hair. "Thanks a lot, Barbara-Jean," I told her as we were leaving. "We're not quite through, so could we borrow the food coloring and some of the wax for a little while? We'd like to work on them later, down at the lake where there's some sand."

"Sure," she answered, "and I'd really like to see those candles when you're done."

"Oh, right!" Debbie said. "If we get some nice ones, we'll lend you the mold. *Ow!*" she cried as I elbowed her.

When we got back to the bunk to change for General Swim, I collected all the stuff and put it in my cubby under my towels.

General Swim comes at about eleven in the morning, the last activity before lunch. It's not lessons or anything; it's just fun-swimming time for the whole camp. And it's not cold out by eleven.

I was so busy thinking about when we'd get a chance to melt the wax and finish the doll and everything, that I swam the whole way out to the float and back without even knowing I did it. I only realized what I had done when I saw Skipper smiling at me and applauding as I climbed up the ladder onto the dock. Hey, I thought, maybe I *will* pass my Intermediate Swim Test this summer!

20

We didn't get to work on the doll the rest of the day. I was hoping we could do it at night after taps, but everybody fell asleep except me. The evening activity had been a rehearsal of all the camp songs in the Rec Hall so we'd sound "happy and enthusiastic", according to Uncle Otto, when we sang for the parents. And it had exhausted everybody.

The next morning, Saturday, was hectic for the counselors. Uncle Otto kept barking orders at them, first at Line-Up, then in the Mess Hall after breakfast, and, finally, he called a counselor meeting during Clean-Up for "last minute details."

When Marcia left the bunk for the meeting, I decided that was the best time to finish the doll. "Not now," Verna wailed, "we haven't finished cleaning."

"Who *cares*, Verna! What's more important?" I wanted to know.

"I don't want my parents to walk into a dirty bunk," Verna insisted.

"Oh, Verna, it'll only take us a few minutes to clean up," Natalie said. "Let's fix the doll. It's more fun."

"Yeah," Debbie said, happy to unload her broom and dustpan. "And, besides, we're not going to be alone around here until tomorrow night or even Monday. I want to try this magic stuff."

"You know," I said, as I took everything out from its place in my cubby, "we're not doing this for *fun*. This is supposed to be justice for Uncle Otto for all the mean things he's done."

"Right," said Debbie, handing over the half-sewn tee-shirt to Verna, along with the needle and thread.

When Verna was through, Iris mixed a green color from the yellow and blue food coloring to dye the shirt. Adele finished the lanyard, which was really cute, and we even had a tiny whistle from a Cracker-Jack box to hang from the end of it.

The moccasins were perfect. We made them out of the soft brown clay, and an extra touch was a tiny piece of string which we made to look like it was laced through the sides of each shoe and tied in front, like the real thing.

The clay mold of the doll looked terrific . . . so much like Uncle Otto it was almost scary. Iris's fingers rounded the cheeks, shaped the lips, narrowed the eyes. Then we were ready for the wax. Since there were no counselors patrolling the Quad, we went out on the porch to light the candle so we could melt the stuff. We held the candle over a small chunk of the wax and let it just drip down until it covered the entire body of the doll. I got burned trying to smooth the hot wax over the features of the face, but I didn't even mind. And, while it was still hot, we smeared some red food coloring into the lips and cheeks to make it more lifelike. One of the last things was getting the hair set into the wax. It was important to fix it the same way Uncle Otto wears his, kind of parted almost in the middle and slicked back on each side.

When it was finished, we stood back to admire it.

"It's amazing," said Verna.

"It's weird," Debbie said.

"It's him," I said, And it *was*. Anyone looking at it would know who it was.

"Goody, what do we do now?" Debbie asked, all excited.

"We do the spell over it," I answered. "What's the spell, Iris?"

"Oh! Oh!" Verna shrieked. "They're here! My parents are here! Oh, look at this mess! Pick it up, pick it up, come on! Oh, come on!"

"Oh, jeez," I groaned, "come off the wall, Verna."

We looked down the road and saw a tan station wagon being directed toward the parking lot that Uncle Otto had set up next to the baseball diamond. "But, please!" Verna was chirping, as she began to gather the scraps of cloth and clay on the porch floor.

"All right, Verna, just take it easy," Adele said,

handing me the finished doll. "Here, Tuffy, hide this in your cubby again."

I went inside and began to help clean. Wouldn't you know Verna's parents would be the first to arrive, practically at dawn!

"Does it look all right? Is it neat?" Verna asked, whirling around.

"It's gorgeous, Verna, go on already," Nat said. And Verna charged out of the bunk toward the parked car.

The bugle blew, announcing First Activity. There were regular activities scheduled on Parents' Weekend, but if your parents showed up, you didn't have to go to them unless you wanted to. A lot of kids went just to show their parents how they were doing and stuff.

We all went out on the porch and watched Verna hug her parents and pull shopping bags out of the car. One great thing about Parents' Weekend is that all the parents bring presents for everyone in the bunk. Mine always brought a big salami, and pounds and pounds of chocolate-covered marshmallow squares from the Nut Shop on Seventy-Second Street in New York City. Anybody can sell chocolate-covered marshmallow squares, but not like the Nut Shop's. They're homemade. My first year at camp I tried to hide them. But that was dumb because they all melted into each other, and everybody found out I hid them and yelled, "BOOOOO!" So now I share.

"Nat, what time are you parents coming?" I asked.

"I dunno. Why?"

"Just wondering." I hoped they would come early. Nat's father always brings about fifty cameras and insisted on taking pictures of all of us doing everything but taking a bath. If he came early he'd get the picture-taking over with and we wouldn't have to be interrupted later. Maybe. Anyway, Natalie loved it; she changed into every outfit she owned.

"Hello, girls," Mrs. Perkins said, smiling as she came up the porch steps.

"Hi." We all smiled back, wondering what she brought.

Verna introduced us, since we hadn't really met at the Terminal. Then she handed out halvah bars and large bags of M & Ms. Debbie dived into them and we knew she'd be busy for the morning.

"Verna, why don't you show us around the camp?" Mr. Perkins suggested.

"Would that be all right, Marcia?" Verna asked.

Marcia said, "Sure, go ahead." One less kid to worry about.

As the Perkinses were leaving, Arnold came in. He was in the middle of the bunk when he saw Verna coming toward him. Instantly, he was outside again, knocking loudly on the screen door. "Oh, Arnold, come in!" I yelled, and he did, this time bumping into Verna on her way out.

"Come on, Adele, they're here," he said.

"Great!" Adele yelled and leaped off her bed. "Listen, girls, we'll come back here first, so stay here awhile, will you?"

"We're going to *my* bunk first," said Arnold.

"We are not, Arnold. I want them to see my friends."

"I want them to see *my* friends!" Arnold whined.

"Listen, Arnold, I'm the oldest and I said we're coming back here first!"

"I'm the youngest. You're supposed to humor me!"

"Arnold, Parents' Weekend will be over by the time you decide whose bunk you're going to first," Nat said.

"Arnold, you like halvah?" I asked.

"Yeah," he said.

"Well, Adele will give you a whole bar of it if you let her bring your parents back here first." I smiled.

"Hey!" Adele said.

"Okay, stand here and argue then," I said, shrugging.

"*Half* a bar," Adele said.

"The whole thing!" Arnold said.

"All *right!*" Adele said finally, and they left together.

"I bet he plays a good Monopoly game," Debbie said, chewing.

The rest of the morning was boring. Natalie, Iris, Debbie and I went to Music, Nature and General Swim. I watched Iris kind of carefully and she seemed okay. She even seemed happy about going out for dinner with my folks. I thought about how I'd feel if my parents weren't coming up. Bad, that's for sure. Definitely bad!

The whole bunk was back for lunch. That was the rule. The parents ate in camp, too, but after the kids. There was always a fantastic lunch on Parents' Weekend. We had fried chicken and mashed potatoes with gravy and rolls! Debbie had an eating *fit!*

As we came out of the Mess Hall, Debbie's parents were standing there. She screamed and ran into their arms. "Come and meet my bunkmates right after lunch!" she yelled. God forbid it should be *before*. Then she went on to describe the lunch. Four weeks away in camp and she talked for ten minutes about the meal they were going to eat!

But we did have to have Rest Hour on Parents' Weekend and now I was beginning to get excited. It wouldn't be long now!

Suddenly the door burst open. A man stood in the doorway and yelled, "Hold it, honey!" and a flashbulb went off. When we stopped blinking, we realized it was Nat's father.

"Hi-i-i-i!" she said, unwrapping her long legs and going to hug him. "Daddy, this is my counselor, Marcia, and this is Iris, and that's Debbie. You know Tuf and Adele. And that's Verna."

"Hello, everyone," Mr. Zinser said, clicking and turning things on his camera. "Say, I've just got to get pictures of you all. How about it, girls." It wasn't a question. He held the camera up to his face, took it down, held it up again. "Now, can I get you in a group? Can you all move over here?"

"*Wait* a minute, Daddy," Nat said. "You just got here. We have all weekend to take pictures. Where's Mom?"

Mr. Zinser looked out the screen door. "Here she comes. She's carrying the rest of my equipment. Be careful, Carol, that's not a Kodak Brownie, you know!"

Mrs. Zinser gave him a funny look. She came into the bunk dragging leather cases, a light meter and a tripod. They always have this stuff with them wherever they go and last year Natalie explained some of it to me. Mrs. Zinser put down the stuff and flopped on Marcia's bed. Nat went through the introductions again, but Mrs. Zinser looked like she just wanted to lie down.

"Mom, what did you bring us?" Nat asked.

"*Film,*" her mother said.

"No, really, did you bring us some food?"

"Yes, dear, but it's in the car. I had to carry your father's equipment and I can't manage everything." She yawned.

"Well, I couldn't have my hands full when I took a surprise picture of my little girl," said Nat's father with a big grin.

"Oh, Daddy," Nat said.

I got up and went to the door. I looked up and down the road. There was no blue Chevy.

Mr. Zinser was setting up his tripod. "All right, girls, now why don't you all move over against that wall."

"George, I think we should take the pictures outside. There's a lot of light, and so much more room," Mrs. Zinser said.

"Carol, I can handle the light and I want a picture inside the bunk. Now girls—" He began to look us all over. I felt like a museum exhibit, but all he was doing was deciding where to place us, according to height and width, and how to put Natalie in the most prominent place. Natalie gleamed and preened . . . She brushed her long hair . . . She swept it up . . . She took it down . . . She put on jeans, shorts, a long skirt. A tee-shirt, a halter, a tunic. A caftan. We posed on Natalie's bed, on the porch, on the Quad . . . "Short ones, up front, tall ones in the back." Mr. Zinser wanted a picture of Iris playing her guitar, but Natalie wanted the picture to be of *her* playing Iris's guitar, so that's what he took. We all smiled at the right times. Iris had an expression on her face that said "I don't believe this," and Debbie never stopped eating. Finally, Nat whined, "Awww, Daddy, you're not through, are you?"

"No, no, honey," Mr. Zinser said. "I want pictures of all of you doing what you do around camp, okay? I won't impose on your time again; I'll just snap candid shots as we go through the weekend."

"Daddy," Nat asked, "how would you like me to tell you about camp?"

"Of course, of course," said her father and they walked out on the porch.

Mrs. Zinser moved over to Natalie's bed and lay down on it.

The bugle blew . . . end of Rest Hour. Adele, Debbie and Verna left quickly to join their parents at the Mess Hall, and Natalie went out with hers.

Marcia said, "Iris, play something on your guitar."

Iris shook her head.

"Iris," I said, "have you ever made up any of your own music?"

"Uh huh."

"Have you ever played any of it . . . In the bunk, I mean?"

Head shake.

"Play some of it now. Please?"

Iris bit on her lower lip and looked at me. Then she stood up and got out the guitar. The song had no words, or, at least, she didn't sing any. She just strummed. It sounded very sweet, half-happy, half-sad. But it had a tune I could remember, knew I would remember. Sometime I'd ask if it had words. Marcia listened with her eyes closed. Maybe she was asleep. Outside we could hear a lot of talking and laughing coming from the Quad. A whole bunch of parents had arrived by then and were strolling around with their kids. I really had an idea of how Iris felt.

I couldn't wait in the bunk anymore so I decided to go down to the edge of the road. At least then I could see the car as soon as it got there.

Cars kept arriving, one after the other. And kids kept running toward them. Once a blue Chevy did pull in, but there was no one in it I knew.

At last! At three forty-five, there they were! I jumped out at the car and almost got run over. Daddy screeched to a halt in the middle of the road. It was a good thing there was no one in back of him. I got into the back of the car and drove with them to the parking lot. "What took you so long? Everybody's been here for hours!"

"Well," Mom said, "Jeannie yelled 'bathroom' right after we got on the highway—"

"Oh, boy!"

"So we had to stop at a gas station, but then she didn't go."

"Jeez!"

"But then she asked to go *again* about a half-an-hour later, so we stopped again, but she still didn't go."

"Aw, Mom!"

"Well, now, honey, I have to give her every chance! You know how long we've waited for her to get the idea."

Daddy leaned over and gave me a big hug, "How's my girl, Bets?"

"Fine, Daddy."

"Bets-see!"

"Hi, Jeannie."

"Bathroom!"

"Oh, Jeannie!" Mom wailed, "you're soaking wet! Look at your dress! Oh, dear!"

"Mom, take her into the Mess Hall. There's a bathroom there and you can change her. Daddy and I can sit outside and wait for you."

The two of us sat down on the wide porch of the Mess Hall. "You like this place, baby?" Daddy asked.

"I do, but something happened this Thursday that I want to talk to you about." Then I told him about Sheila and how she got fired. Daddy didn't say a word until I was finished.

"I gather you feel Uncle Otto was unfair, right?"

"Right."

"You liked Sheila a lot."

"I sure did. We all did."

He leaned back against the wooden railing. "You know, there is a curfew for a good reason, Bets."

"I know, but Sheila had a good reason for not making it."

"Wouldn't it have been much better if she had called from the hospital? Then no one would have worried."

"I bet he would have fired her anyway. He never believes anyone. He just walks away without listening."

"But we don't know what he believes, do we?" Daddy said. "Sheila should have called. Then we could talk about fair and unfair."

"Daddy, she thought of calling, but she figured she could make it back in time. She didn't know she was that sick."

"Maybe Uncle Otto was a little tough," he said, "but I can see his side. He was up all night not knowing what happened to her. He is responsible for her, even though she's an employee."

"Daddy," I said, feeling my face suddenly get hot, "don't take *his* side."

"Betsy, I'm not taking sides," he said. "I'm only trying to show you that there *is* another side of the story and, quite possibly, a reasonable one."

"It isn't reasonable! He hasn't been reasonable about anything all summer. Sheila was the nicest counselor I ever had. Come on, you're the one who taught me about fairness and always giving the other person a chance."

"That's right," Daddy said. "Are you doing that for Uncle Otto?"

"Do you know how many times we tried to talk to him?" I was beginning to yell a little. I didn't want to yell at Daddy; he just got there and I hadn't seen him for a whole month.

"Look, Betsy," he said, putting an arm around my shoulder, "you're upset now because you're missing Sheila. She's only been gone for a couple of days."

"I wanted you to talk with her."

"I know. But, look, when you get home, you can call her and invite her to dinner. We'll talk with her. Promise me you'll think about the other fellow's side when you cool down. Maybe you'll get to feel a little better about the whole situation."

I dug a hole in the dirt with the toe of my shoe. "I won't cool down," I mumbled.

Mom and Jeannie came out just then and we took a walk up to the bunk. "Iris is coming to dinner with us tonight, isn't she?" Mom asked.

"Yeah," I said, and started to put Uncle Otto out of my mind.

Everyone was in our bunk except Verna and her parents, and Iris. Mom and Dad were glad to see the Zinsers and the Brodys again. And Debbie's parents were very nice. They were the only ones who didn't bring food! But they brought us yo-yos, two decks of cards and little boxes of note paper. I hid the marshmallow squares. I didn't mind passing them out to my friends, but if all the parents were going to eat them too, that would be a drag.

"Where's Iris?" I asked Marcia.

"She went for a walk."

"Did she say when she'd be back?"

"No, Tuffy. She's okay. She'll be back."

Nat's father dragged us all out on the porch for a group picture with our parents, and then I took Mom and Dad around the camp. They really liked the lake. I wondered if Mom liked it enough for a second year.

"Dave," Mom said, "we haven't met the Head Counselor yet. Shouldn't we find him? Or is it *her?*"

"It's *him.* Don't meet him, Mom."

"Why not?"

"There are nicer people to meet. Forget him."

"*Jeannie,* don't walk into the lake! Oh, by the way, Betsy, here are your nose plugs."

"Wow, you remembered! Thanks."

"It's okay, Sylvia," Daddy said. "There'll be plenty of time to meet some of the people later. Meanwhile, Bets, where do you think we're having dinner tonight?"

"Where?"

"Well, we stopped in Honesdale on our way—"

"Because Jeannie asked to go again," Mom said.

"But she didn't," said Dad. "Anyway, there was a lovely old hotel there, The Brighton Arms. We went in, and their dining room is just beautiful. We thought you and Iris would enjoy it."

"That reminds me, where *is* Iris? Maybe I should have her paged over the loudspeaker."

"All right," Daddy said, "do that. It's five-thirty now and we don't want to keep you out too late. You do have to be back for Evening Activity, don't you?"

It was a special Evening Activity for the parents. The counselors were putting on a variety show. Sheila was supposed to have had a funny part in it and a song, but now that part was out.

Mom was pulling Jeannie out of a canoe when I left to go back to the Quad. If I had to ask Uncle Otto to page Iris, I wanted to do it without Mom and Dad there. The further I kept them apart, the better. Luckily he wasn't in the H.C. shack, but Aunt Louise was. I asked her to do the paging and she did.

"Iris Connor: Please report to the H.C. shack. Iris Connor: Report to the H.C. shack now, please."

I went outside and waited . . . And waited. No Iris. Aunt Louise paged her again five minutes later . . . No Iris. Then I got scared.

21

I figured there were two possibilities: Iris either left camp, and, if she did, there was nothing I could do. Or she was somewhere *in* camp and, if so, where would she be? If she left camp, maybe Daddy could drive down the road to Honesdale and see if she was trying to hitch a ride. But where would she hitch to? Home to a housekeeper? You can't hitch to Paris. No, she wouldn't leave. That would be dumb, and Iris wasn't dumb. She had to be somewhere around camp.

I raced back to Bunk Ten. The other girls were there, dressing for dinner. Hardly anyone would be in camp at dinnertime.

"Has Iris come back?" I asked.

Marcia came in from the john, brushing her teeth. She talked to me through a mouthful of toothpaste and I couldn't understand her.

"She says Iris took her guitar," Adele translated, fastening a silver necklace. "So she must have gone to some quiet place where she could be alone."

I had an idea and took off, with Marcia trying to yell at me from the porch, her mouth still foaming. The idea was the Arts and Crafts shack. It was an out-of-the-way, enclosed place, and I knew how much she liked it.

I heard the guitar before I even got close. What a relief! I sat down on the grass and took a few deep breaths before I went in.

She didn't even look up when I pushed the door open. "Hi," she said, and went on strumming. She was playing "Bob Dylan's Dream."

"Come on, Iris, we have to go," I said quietly.

"You go. I just feel like sitting here."

"No, come on. They know you're missing."

"You reported me missing?" She stopped playing.

I was miserable. "I had you paged. Aunt Louise did it. She knows you're gone. Then I looked for you in the bunk, so Marcia knows, too. She was screaming at me when I took off to come here. Oh, God, I'm sorry! I just didn't know where you were. I got scared."

"No, it's my fault . . . I heard the page."

I sat down on one of the stools. "Then why didn't you answer? We were ready to go out to dinner."

"I know."

"Oh."

"No, it isn't you, Tuffy," she said. "I just couldn't take it with so many parents . . . And Mr. Zinser snapping pictures all over the place."

"I understand that. I really do! But now you've got to come with me. You can't stay here and face Aunt Louise and Uncle Otto all by yourself. My dad will be with us. Uncle Otto wouldn't dare yell at you with him there."

"I don't want to see anybody," she said unhappily.

"You won't have to. We'll leave camp right now. Mom and Dad picked this real nice place for us to have dinner. Please, Iris."

"What about this?" she asked, looking down at her guitar.

"We'll take it. You won't even have to go back to the bunk to put it away."

"No," she said, "that's no good. If they're worried, they've got to know I'm here. I don't want to get in real trouble."

We decided to go to the H.C. shack first, and they were all there, Mom, Dad, Jeannie, Uncle Otto, Aunt Louise and Marcia. Well, it saved me a bunch of introductions.

"Hi, folks!" I said.

"Where were you, Iris?" Uncle Otto asked. Every time he lowers his voice I get nervous. Well, at least Daddy would see him in action.

I started to say, "She was—"

"Iris?" said Uncle Otto.

"I was by myself," Iris said.

"Why didn't you answer your page?"

"I wanted to stay by myself."

"You had a lot of people worried."

"I'm sorry."

"Come on, Iris," Mom said. "You come out with us now. You're going to feel a whole lot better when you've had a real good dinner." And she put her arm around Iris and walked her away. Good old Mom!

She reached up and shook Uncle Otto's hand. I split for the car. "Thank you," I heard Dad say, "we'll take care of her now." And we headed for the car.

Daddy had us laughing in a few minutes. It was going to be okay. We had Iris's guitar with us and Mom and Dad asked about it. On the way into town, I told them how well Iris played and how she even wrote her own songs. "And you mean to say," Mom said, "that after four weeks no one except your bunkmates knows you have this talent!"

Iris smiled.

"Well, I just think that's dreadful. Isn't there some kind of talent show? Every camp has one. I remember last year, Betsy, you sang—"

"Yes," I interrupted, "there is. It's a musicale, and it's this Thursday night. Kids are going to sing and dance and play instruments. Arnold's bunk is doing a barber shop quartet."

"And you're not going to be in it, Iris?" Dad asked.

"Oh, no," she said softly.

"I think it would do you and Camp Ma-Sha-Na a lot of good if you'd sing in that musicale," Dad said.

"I couldn't do that," Iris said.

"Of course you could," I said. "You know you

sing rings around anybody we've heard this summer, including Paul. You'd be terrific, you don't have to worry about that."

"But I couldn't sing in front of people."

"What people, a bunch of kids younger than you? Tell you what, we'll be on the stage with you. We'll sing the stuff we always sing around the bunk, 'St. James Infirmary' and 'I'm in Love with a Big Blue Frog' and stuff like that. We'll do it as a bunk. Come on, what do you say?"

"I'll think about it." She smiled as the car swung into the hotel parking lot.

"Good," I said, "it's settled."

The hotel *was* really beautiful and there was a table set up for us, even though we were late. A lot of kids from camp were there with their parents. They were scattered all over the dining room. We waved to them and they waved back. It was funny to see them in a different place, in different clothes. I hadn't had a chance to change and neither had Iris. We were still in jeans. Good thing my folks don't care about things like that. I pulled up a chair but it was caught on something. I yanked at it.

"Hey!" someone said. "You're pulling my sweater!" I turned around, ready for a fight. It was Alex. He was right at the next table with his parents and some little kid about Jeannie's age. His sweater was hooked around the back of my chair.

"Sorry," I said, "I didn't see it there."

"You shoulda looked," he said, frowning.

"Your canoeing is better than your manners. I *said* I was sorry."

"Okay, but you looked like you were going to punch me one just now."

I grinned. "In front of your parents? Never."

He laughed.

Jeannie pointed at the little kid at Alex's table. "*Baby!*" she yelled.

"I'm not a baby," the kid said, "I'm a big boy!"

"Who's he, your brother?" I asked Alex.

"Yeah, his name is B.G. He's four."

"B.G.?"

"Benjamin Gordon."

"Oh."

Just then the waiter brought the menus. Iris and I both ordered lobster tails and the waiter brought us bibs.

"Just like camp, right, Iris?" I said.

"Oh, yeah," she said, "cloth napkins, waiters, glasses with ice water—"

"And *lobster*," I added. "We have lobster at least twice a week."

"We sure do," said Iris, "only they call it chipped beef. They don't want to spoil us."

Daddy laughed. He ordered roast beef for himself and Mom, and Jeannie asked for a hot dog. We ordered her chopped steak.

"Want to see the *baby!*" Jeannie squealed and climbed out of her bumper seat.

"No, Jeannie," Mom said, making a grab for her and missing.

"I'm not a baby," B.G. yelled, "I'm a big boy!"

Jeannie ran over to B.G. and poked at him, smiling. B.G. hit Jeannie with his hard roll.

"Wahhhhhh!" hollered Jeannie. Dad was out of his seat like a shot. "Baby hit me," she sobbed. By now the whole dining room was staring at us.

"I'm not a baby, I'm a big boy!"

Alex's mother kept saying, "Of course you're a big boy, honey, you're a *big* boy!"

"Alex," I said, "your brother hits little girls."

"He learned that from me," said Alex.

"Alexander, take your brother to the little boys' room, won't you, dear?" his mother asked.

"Oh," Mom said, "I'd better take Jeannie, too."

I jumped up. "I'll do it. Let me take her." And, kind of surprising myself, I grabbed Jeannie and took off after Alex and B.G.

"Alex, wait," I called.

"What?"

"Well, I had an idea—"

"I can't wait to hear it," he said, still walking.

"No, look, I want to try something. Is B.G. trained?"

"Is he *what?*"

"Toilet-trained."

"Sure he is."

"Well, Jeannie isn't, and I was wondering . . . Maybe if she went in with him to the bathroom. I mean, maybe if she saw how the big kids do it—"

"You want B.G. to go in the Men's Room with her?"

"Well at that age it doesn't matter. They're not going to be staring at each other, for God's sake.

Jeannie isn't even three yet. Just let her watch how B.G. does it . . . You know, not in his pants. Look, I'll take them both in the Ladies' Room. Okay?"

"Sure," he said, "take 'em. I'll wait here."

I went in. "Hey, B.G., did you say you're a big boy now?"

"I'm not a baby, I'm a big—"

"*Boy*. Right! I know," I said. "Okay, B.G., show baby Jeannie how the big kids go to the bathroom. You don't go in your pants anymore, do you?"

"No-o-o-o," he said, "I go to the potty. I'm a big—"

"Right, B.G. Now Jeannie, you just watch B.G. See? His pants are dry because he goes to the potty, not in his pants. Now watch!"

B.G. pulled down his little short pants and went. And, as soon as he did it, I knew I had made a big mistake. Jeannie walked right over to the toilet next to him, pulled down her pants, stood there and peed down her leg.

I mopped her up with paper towels, and wiped her shoes. Then I stood the two of them up against the wall.

"Now look, you two, especially you, Jeannie, I want you to forget everything I said in here, okay? Just forget it. Forget the whole thing. You don't go like B.G., okay, Jeannie? You're a girl, so you have to sit down. B.G. stands up. Look, just forget it, okay?"

Alex was waiting outside for us. "Did she get the idea?" he asked.

"She got it," I said.

"What'd you order for dinner?" he asked.

"Lobster tails. How about you?"

"Oh yeah, me too. Never see anything like that at camp. At home, either!"

"Thanks for letting me borrow your brother," I said when we got to our tables.

"Oh, any time," he smiled. "You can have him!"

I looked at Iris. She was smiling, laughing. I never saw her so—relaxed. That was it, *relaxed*.

"What're you talking about?" I asked, lifting Jeannie into her chair.

"Oh, I was just wondering," Iris said, "how a West Hempstead fly can write letters from Groton, Connecticut."

I looked at Daddy and he laughed.

"Tuffy, what's this?" Marcia was standing at my cubby door. I was getting into my pajamas after the dinner and the counselors' variety show. Marcia was pointing to a little arm and a little leg sticking out from my towel.

"What are you doing in my cubby?" I asked.

"I thought," she said evenly, "that this was your towel. It was left on my bed and I was putting it in with your things."

"It's not my towel," I said.

"Well, neither is *this*," said Marcia.

I went over to my cubby and tucked the doll back in. Just touching it made me angry again. "It's a surprise," I told her. "For my little sister. It's just a doll I made. I'm not through with it yet."

22

We had services the next morning, just like we do every Sunday. Everyone wears a white tee-shirt and white shorts. And they read some stuff from a Bible that won't offend anyone from any religion, and then somebody tells a story that's supposed to have a moral in it. That's what they call the sermon. Most of the parents liked it; mine could take it or leave it. We're not much into religion. Jeannie sat with B.G. and was really very good, for *her*. The only thing she did was throw her plastic Charlie the Tuna across the aisle. It hit Arnold on the back of the neck. But that was okay, because only Arnold got in trouble for yelling, not Jeannie.

The rest of the day was weird. There were some activities scheduled but nobody went to any. All the parents were leaving at different times. Kids whose parents left early just wandered around camp by themselves or in groups. The rest of us, I think, felt a little funny because our parents were still hanging around.

I think I felt the weirdest of all. I really hated to see Mom and Dad go, but Jeannie was getting to be a drag. Besides I wanted our bunk to be alone, so we could get back to the doll. I think Iris was sorrier than I was when they finally pulled out of the parking lot and started down the camp road. We both stood at the side of the road and waved, but she stayed there longer than I did.

Uncle Otto announced an early dinner, probably to get rid of some of the late-leaving parents. It worked. By five o'clock, all the visitors were gone.

Dinnertime was back to normal, franks and beans. We were just getting up to leave when Uncle Otto came over to the table. "Bunk Ten, you may leave the dining room. But, Iris, I want you to stay," he said.

Just as I was about to open my mouth, Natalie dug her nails into my arm and pushed me out. Then we all sat down on the porch of the Mess Hall to wait.

"Why'd you do that?" I asked Natalie.

"Because this isn't the time to say anything, Tuffy," she said. "You never know when to be quiet."

"Yes," Verna said, "wait until he talks to her. Maybe he won't do anything."

"Marcia, you probably should have stayed in there with her. You have an excuse; you're her counselor."

"No, Tuffy, if he wanted me there, he would have said so. Just wait and see what happens."

Pretty soon Iris came out, alone. She was all red in the face. We got up quickly so we could walk away from there fast and not be overheard. Everyone crowded around Iris, but she just kept walking and not saying anything. Each time one of us would ask a question, she would stop and walk in another direction, sort of to shake us off, like flies. Finally Marcia said, "Listen, just leave her alone. She doesn't want to talk now. Let her go back to the bunk by herself, and maybe she'll tell you about it later."

There wasn't any choice, so we walked over to the tennis court and sat down on the red clay ground. In our white shorts.

"Anybody want to make a little bet on what Uncle Bigfoot said?" Debbie asked.

"It's not funny, Debbie."

"I know it's not funny, but since Iris won't tell us, we can only guess. He couldn't send her home because there isn't anyone there to take care of her, so it's not that drastic."

Nat said, "I bet he grounded her, like he did me."

"No, she was too upset," Adele said. "It had to be worse than that."

"She happens to be very sensitive," I told them. "She could get very upset even if he just yelled at her, so it could be anything."

"I bet it's 'no canteen' for a week," Debbie said.

"No, Debbie, that'd be your punishment," said Natalie. "Nobody else would care about 'no canteen'."

"Arnold would," Adele said.

"Listen, I can't stand it anymore. You guys sit

here and roll around in the clay, I'm going back to the bunk!" And I got up and ran all the way.

Marcia was on the porch and, with a toss of her head, told me that Iris was inside.

She was lying down, staring at the roof. "I really want to know what happened," I said, sitting on my own bed and facing her.

"Oh, nothing, really, Tuffy. He just told me I scared everybody and how awful it would have looked if a lot of parents found out some kid ran away from camp on Parents' Weekend."

"How awful it would have *looked!*"

"Yeah, and he grounded me."

"From what?"

"From Evening Activity for five days."

"Five days? But Thursday is the musicale!"

"Well, I'm not complaining about that; I wouldn't have done it anyway," she said. "He just embarrassed me and made me feel bad, but I'm okay now."

I don't even remember running out of the bunk. I was out of there and across the Quad so fast it was like I was shot from a gun. All I could think of was that it was taking so long to reach Uncle Otto's cabin that I'd never get there. It seemed farther away than China. And I think I must have been crying, because I had to blink my eyes a lot to see where I was going. I didn't even knock; I couldn't take the time. I couldn't take my mind off what I was thinking, or I wouldn't have been able to say anything at all. It's a good thing they weren't undressed or anything when I charged right in and started yelling from the second my foot was over the threshhold.

"How *could* you do that to her?" I screamed. "You don't have any heart *at all!* Don't you know how it *feels* when everybody in the whole world's parents come up to visit and yours *don't* and *never have?* Don't you *care* what somebody thinks when they're watching a father who wants to take a thousand pictures of his little girl while your *own* father is taking pictures of the *Eiffel Tower?* You don't think of anything but your dumb awards and schedules, schedules, *schedules!* You don't care at all about how a person feels *inside.* And *just* when we were beginning to get Iris to think about finally performing and playing her music for the camp, which she wouldn't have even *considered* a month ago, you come in like the Wicked Witch of the West and *ground* her from the musicale!" I was beginning to run out of steam but I hated to let go, because I was finally getting it all out. Neither Uncle Otto nor Aunt Louise had taken their eyes off me even for a second, and I didn't want to lose their attention. I had this feeling that if I stopped talking he would kill me, so I kept on hollering words until I choked and started to cry. I saw them look away from me and at each other and, when they did that, I just split.

As soon as I was out of here, I knew I had better sit down. My legs were really rubbery and my head hurt. I went over to the edge of the yard near the thick trees, picked out the thickest, and collapsed. I started to take deep breaths because that's what you're supposed to do if you feel faint, but it didn't work because I fainted anyway. Or maybe I fell asleep, I don't know, but the next thing I knew it was dark.

I rubbed my eyes and walked to where I could get a view of some of the camp. I wanted to see if I could figure out what time it was. As I got closer to the Quad, I could see a lot of people moving around, which meant that the call for Evening Activity hadn't been played yet. Then I remembered . . . There was no Evening Activity tonight, just Bunk Games. Uncle Otto had said he wanted us to rest up from the busy weekend, but we all knew it was Uncle Otto who wanted to rest.

Bunk Games . . . I knew what our Bunk Game would be. I looked at the sky and staring down at me was a full moon.

23

When I got to the bunk, things were quiet. Each girl was on her own bed. Debbie was playing solitaire between bites of my marshmallow squares; Nat was filing her nails; Adele was reading a magazine; Verna was re-folding her sweaters; and Iris was staring at the ceiling . . . A typical evening-at-home. Marcia was on her bed reading *Fear of Flying* and paying no attention to anyone. This was the time.

"Hello!" I said. Everyone jumped.

"Oh, hi," Adele said, and went back to her magazine. "Where were you?"

"Oh, just around. Listen, everybody, it's a good time to work on our project."

Nat looked up, interested, "Oh! Yeah! That's a good idea. Come on, girls."

"What project?" Debbie asked.

"*You* know," Nat said, glaring at her.

"Why don't we go out on the porch?" I suggested.

Slowly, they all put down their things and began to get up.

"What project?" Marcia said, but she didn't look up from her book.

"Just some candles and things we were making. It's something to do," I answered. And I began to take the things out of my cubby and hand them to each girl as she slipped out the door.

"Okay," Marcia said, still glued to the book. "But don't go off the porch. We're all supposed to stay at our bunks tonight."

"Right."

When I got out, they had the stuff spread out on Trunk Number Two. "All right, Iris," I said. "What's the spell?"

"Tuffy, I told you, I never did this before. This is your game. I'm just a helper."

"Well, help, then. Get the book that has the spell."

She came out with one of her books and we looked all through it. It told about the dolls and other kinds of voodoo magic, like love potions and stuff, but no spells. "We're going to have to make up a spell," I announced.

"That's no good!" Debbie said.

"You mean we went through all this for nothing?" Natalie asked.

"No. Any spell will do as long as we mean it. The doll's the important thing," I insisted. "Besides, look! There's a full moon! Everybody knows weird things happen during a full moon."

"What weird things?" Verna asked.

"Boy, Verna, don't you ever watch T.V.? Haven't

you ever seen 'Return of the Vampire' or 'Kiss of Evil' or even 'Frankenstein Meets the Wolfman'? Magic things happen on the night of a full moon. Now you better believe it, or this won't work."

I put the doll on the floor of the porch and looked up at Iris. "Okay, what now?"

"Well, I guess you have to draw the magic circle," Iris said.

"Circle?"

"Yes, around the doll. Dip your finger in the food coloring and paint it on the floor."

"What color?" I asked.

"Yellow," she answered.

"Why yellow?"

"I like yellow."

"Oh."

"Now, we have to chant," Iris said.

"What do we chant?" Adele asked.

"We have to chant magic words. Anybody know any magic words?"

"How about 'abra cadabra'?" Verna offered.

I glared at her. "Get another book, Iris."

Iris went in and came back with another book. I snatched it and began to pore through it.

"Okay, here's something! Now listen to this." I read. " 'These cryptic words were chanted when one hundred fifty-seven persons were burned as witches in the province of Wurzberg between 1627 and 1629:

Lalle, Bachera, Magotte, Baphia, Dajam,
Vagoth, Heneche, Ammi Nagaz, Adomator,

Raphael Immanuel Christus, Tetragrammaton, Agra Jod Loi. Konig! Konig!'"

"'Konig, Konig'?" said Debbie.

"Tuffy, that sounds like nonsense!" Adele said.

"I bet you didn't even pronounce it right," Nat said. "It sounded funny."

"Listen, those are magic words. They sound a lot better than 'abra cadabra'!" I said.

"Well," Iris said, looking at the page, "that incantation's no good anyway."

"Why not?" I asked. I already liked the sound of it.

"Because it's used for raising the Devil in the form of a goat. Here, look for yourself."

"'The following invocation raised the Devil in the form of a goat.' Nuts! All right, we'll look for something else."

I thumbed through the book again.

Each chapter had a little verse to introduce it. Maybe one of those would do ... "Got one! Listen:

'Thus from the inmost shrine speaks the Sibyl of Cumae,
Equivokes fearful she chants, the cavern resounding,
Truth in obscurity veiled; Apollo her madness
Stirs with his reins, and rowels his goad in her breast.'

By Virgil," I finished. "How does that grab you?"

"What does it mean?" Debbie asked.

"How should I know? It's got the word 'chant' in it."

"What does 'rowel his goad in her breast' mean?" Nat wanted to know.

"I don't know."

"Let's look it up. It sounds dirty!"

"Natalie, do you like it or not?"

"I don't know what it *means*, Tuf! How do I know if I like it?"

"All *right!* I'm going to try one more time." They all sighed and looked bored. I turned the pages carefully, checking each chapter head. Finally, I came to one I liked. "All right, here's a poem by Robert Burns about witches. Now you don't have to understand every word of it as long as it sounds right, got it? Okay, listen:

> 'Warlocks and witches in a dance;
> Nae cotillion brent-new frae France,
> But hornpipes, jigs, strathspeys, and reels
> Put life and mettle in their heels:
> A winnock bunker in the east,
> There sat Auld Nick in shape o' beast;
> A towsie tyke, black, grim, and large,
> To gie them music was his charge;
> He screwed the pipes and gart them skirl,
> Till roof and rafters a' did dirl.'

What do you think?"

"What's a 'winnock bunker'?" Debbie asked.

"Debbie, I told you, it doesn't matter if we don't understand a few words."

"I didn't understand *any* words," she said.

"What does it mean, 'he screwed the pipes'?" Nat wanted to know.

"*Stop!*" I held up my hands. "Everybody be quiet. We need a chant for the spell and now we've got a chant. It's probably better if we *don't* understand it. Now we're going to hold the book over the magic circle, like this, and we're all going to read this poem out loud in a low voice, like we were chanting. Does everybody have that?"

Everybody had it. We all started moving into a semi-circle so we could see the words on the page. I took what was left of the candle and lit it, then put it at the head of the doll. Then we all settled back in a cross-legged position, "Everybody ready?" I asked.

"Yes, but you're holding the book directly over the candle," said Iris.

"Well, if I move it down, I can't read."

"Wait, I'll get a flashlight," Adele said.

"What are you girls doing out there?" Marcia called.

"Telling ghost stories," I answered.

"Oh."

Adele got the flashlight and once again we were all in place. "I'll count to three and we'll all start chanting. One . . . Two . . . Three. 'Warlocks and witches in a dance—'" We chanted the whole thing. "Again," I whispered when we finished. "We have to do it three times."

"Who said so?" Debbie asked.

"*I* said so. Now don't break the spell. Keep chanting."

We got through it three times, and I put the book down. "Now what?" whispered Debbie.

"Now we stick the pin in."

"You mean like in the story?" Verna asked. "In the heart?"

I stopped, with the pin in my hand. In the *heart!* I couldn't stick it in the heart. What if something really happened? Besides, I already had gotten a lot of my feelings out when I hollered at him before in his cabin.

"Well, go on, stick it!" Nat said. "I'm getting cold."

But still, fair was fair . . . He deserved a punishment . . . But oh, wow, in the heart? I raised the pin and plunged it into the right ankle of the doll.

"The ankle?" Debbie said.

"The ankle!" Nat started to laugh, so did Adele. Pretty soon we were all rolling around the porch. Marcia started out of the bunk. As I saw her opening the screen door, I quickly sat up in front of the circle so she couldn't see it.

"Hey, what's so funny?" she asked.

"Just a joke Debbie told," said Adele. "It was really hysterical!" We were wiping our eyes.

"Tell it to me," Marcia said.

"Well, you had to be here to appreciate it," Debbie said. "We'll be right in, Marcia. We're going to pick up some of our Arts and Crafts stuff."

I lifted the doll carefully and put it into a bag, with the pin still sticking out of the ankle.

As we were going into the bunk, Debbie took my arm. "You know what, Tuf?"

"What?"

"I really liked that 'Konig, Konig' chant better."

24

The very next morning, right after Line-Up and Flag-Raising, Uncle Otto tripped and fell on a step leading into the Mess Hall. Everyone who wasn't already inside saw it, including us.

Verna screamed, but the rest of us just stared. Everyone's mouth was open as we looked at each other's faces. "I don't believe it," Natalie whispered. "He's doing it on purpose to scare us."

"Natalie, did you just hear yourself?" Adele asked.

"That's right, how could he know?" Nat said, chewing her knuckle. Iris was very pale and continued to stare at Uncle Otto, who had rolled to a sitting position and was now clutching his right leg.

"Are you going to faint?" I asked. She shook her head. "It works, Iris! It really works!"

Again she shook her head. "Freaky coincidence," she said.

"*Too* freaky, Iris! It works!"

Two counselors were helping Uncle Otto to his feet. Our last glimpse, as we went into breakfast, was of Uncle Otto being helped toward the infirmary, his right leg bent at the knee.

I couldn't eat breakfast. The noisy Mess Hall activity was like a dull blur in my head. All I could think was that I made magic happen. I made magic *happen!* Did I really? Or was it a coincidence? But, wait a minute, if it wasn't a coincidence, then I *hurt* somebody. Oh, God! What if I had stuck the pin in the heart, like we were going to do? And what do I do with the doll now?

We walked back to the bunk after breakfast in a huddle. "What do we do with the doll?" I wanted to know.

"Well, I guess we're finished with it," Adele said.

"I know, but if we throw it away or bury it, something really awful might happen," I said. "What do you think, Iris?"

"I never read anything about what they did with the doll after they were through with it."

"Let's ask the Major," Nat said.

"We can't. He'll suspect something."

"What can he suspect if we just ask him a question?"

"We're not bringing outsiders into this!" I insisted.

"Well, then," Nat said, "you're risking a man's life."

"Don't be dramatic, Natalie!" But, at the same time, who could take a chance? Still, I couldn't ask anyone about it. Think, now, I thought. Be logical.

We made the doll to look like Uncle Otto. Now we *un*make the doll. When we got back to the bunk, I took the bag out from under my bed and gently put the doll down on my pillow. The first thing I did was take out the pin. Then I began to take off the clothes carefully, piece by piece. Next, the hairs came out of the head. I couldn't help wincing as I pulled out each one. All the girls watched, offering cute bits of advice, like . . . "Ooh, be careful how you take off his shirt!" . . . "Watch how you take off his shoe, you'll hurt him!"

When we finally got him stripped and bald, I said, "All right, now we've got to change the shape of his face."

"Oh, Tuf, you'll kill him!" Adele whined.

"No, look, it's not *him* anymore. It's somebody else. Somebody who's not real; somebody we don't know. Listen, why don't we say the chant backwards? That'll undo the spell."

Debbie wanted to know how it would undo the spell.

"Because I *said* so," I yelled. "Now quick, get in the same places on the floor you were in last night."

We put the naked doll on the floor in another magic circle. Iris got the book and we read the whole poem backwards over the doll three times. We felt like idiots, but I was taking no chances.

> "Dirl did a' rafters and roof till
> Skirl them gart and pipes the screwed he
> Charge his was music them gie to
> Large and grim, black, tyke towsie a

Beast o' shape in Nick Auld sat there
East the in bunker winnock a
Heels their in mettle and life put
Reels and strathspeys, jigs, hornpipes but
France frae new-brent cotillion nae
Dance a in witches and warlocks."

By the third time, we were babbling at each other,
and Adele was having an allergy attack. All those
nutsy words probably clogged her sinuses. Debbie
and Natalie were giggling through it all, but Iris,
Verna and I really tried to read it straight and we
got through it somehow.

Then, just to be on the safe side, I took one of
my pillowcases and went outside, deep into the
woods in back of the bunks. I wrapped the doll
warmly and neatly in the pillowcase, making sure
not to cover its mouth and nose, and I made a nice
soft bed for it in some pine needles. I left it there,
with a thick branch directly over it to keep out bad
weather. Then I knelt down, made up some kind
of prayer, crossed myself and walked away backwards. I don't know why I did any of that, except
that the good guys kept crossing themselves in
"Kiss of Evil", so I figured that was a good thing to
do. And in all the movies any smart guy knows you
don't turn your back on the Devil, so that's why I
walked backwards. Now, all we could do was hope
he got better fast!

During Rest Hour, Aunt Louise brought the mail
as usual. Nat got a card from some boy, but the

rest of us didn't get anything. I guess because we just saw our parents yesterday. "How's Uncle Otto?" Debbie asked. None of us looked at Aunt Louise. She must have thought that was kind of strange.

"Oh, just fine, thanks, Debbie."

Then we looked up. "He's *fine?*" Natalie asked.

"Yes, it only turned out to be a bad sprain, not a break. We took him to the hospital in the van right after it happened and we just got back a little while ago. He'll have to stay off his foot for awhile, but he'll be up and around in no time." Aunt Louise smiled, "I'll give him your regards." But she didn't look at me.

"The reverse spell is working," I said when she left. "Can you imagine if we had stuck the pin in the heart the way we were going to?"

"Yeah," Nat said. "He would have tripped and fallen on his heart!"

"No, Nat, it's not funny. The man really got hurt because of us."

"Do you really think so, Tuffy?" Adele asked, "I mean *really?* And anyway, isn't that what we started out to do, to hurt him with the doll, just like in the story?"

"I don't know," I said. "I guess so."

"Well, I know what we're going to do next!" announced Natalie.

"What?" Debbie asked.

"We're going to try one more trick to make sure this wasn't a fluke, and then we'll go to work on individual requests!"

"What are you tal

"We're going to lo

book and try it. Let's c

works as well as this or

magic stuff, Tuffy, you

spell you picked was just

else we can do!"

I hadn't even thought a

magic. "I don't know if I wa

"What do you mean? Of c

Nat yelled.

"Hold it, Natalie, I want to th

"Leave her alone, Natalie," Iris

"What?"

"I said, 'leave her alone'."

Nat stood up, "I don't understand

whole thing started with you and th

"I didn't start anything," Iris said.

a bunch of books. I didn't tell you to

with them."

"Well, still—" Nat muttered.

We let it drop, but Nat began to change

me. Instead of our usual joking put-downs

other, she insisted on being as sweet as sug

"Come on, Tuf, let's take a walk!" . . . "Let

play handball, just you and me!" . . . And she a

ally pushed Verna out of the way so she could

next to me that night at dinner. Except for Na

personality change, the day was very relaxed, wit

Uncle Otto nowhere to be seen. I wondered how

long it took a sprained ankle to heal.

...ing about?" I asked.

...k up something else in ...

...o another spell and see if it

...e did. You're good at this

...eally made it work. The

...right. *Now* let's see what

...bout doing any more

...t to," I said.

...ourse you want to,"

...ink about it!"

...said.

...you, Iris. This

...ose books!"

"I just have

...experiment

...toward

...of each

...ar . . .

...'s go

...ctu-

...sit

...'s

...h

...of

...other

...so nice

...girls were

...was the way

...I left everybody

...as hot, so some kids

...n't there, since he was

...w, but some of the Spe-

...own on the dock to super-

...y of boats and canoes and I

...anted to do, go canoeing and

...magic or Uncle Otto or Nat or

...ut the best aluminum canoe, the one

...east dents in it, and stepped in with my

...I decided to paddle to the west end of the

...and watch the sunset all by myself. I pushed

off with the paddle, but the canoe didn't move. I jammed the paddle into the mud and rocked my body forward but the canoe still didn't move. Then someone behind me laughed. I turned around and saw Alex with his foot in my canoe.

"You're not so tough," he said. "Can't you get your canoe out of the mud?"

"Not with a size sixteen foot in it, I can't. Why don't you put the rest of it in here and ride with me?" I offered.

"There are plenty of other canoes," he said.

"Well, then get in one and get your foot out of mine."

"I couldn't do that. You can't even move this one away from the shore. You need help!" And he got in the back of my canoe.

"Where are you going?" he asked.

"West. To watch the sun go down."

"I've got a better idea," he said. "My counselor, Paul, said that Camp Alana is having sailboat races tonight. They're only about a mile from us on this lake. Let's head south and maybe we could watch them."

"Okay, great," I said. "By the way, my sister had a good time with your brother last weekend."

"Oh, yeah?"

That was it for conversation until we had paddled for about fifteen minutes. Then we saw a sail heading away from shore.

"Look," Alex called, "that must be part of the race. Paddle faster!"

We did, but all we saw was that one sail in the

distance. Back at camp I heard the bugle blow back-to-the-bunk for Evening Activity.

"Alex," I said, "we've got to go back."

"Aw, come on, we're just getting there. We won't get in trouble. Uncle Otto's foot is up over his head somewhere."

"I know, but just the same, we've got to go back. I'm really sorry, but if you only knew what could happen if one more person from our bunk got lost!"

"Okay, okay, let's go. I'll race you back," he laughed.

It *was* a good thing we didn't stay on the lake. As soon as I reached the bunk, Marcia came out to meet me.

"Tuffy," she said, "Uncle Otto wants to see our whole bunk in his cabin . . . Right now, before Evening Activity."

We all held our breath walking to his cabin. Adele said, "He knows! He's going to send us home for breaking his ankle. What'll I tell my mother?"

Natalie said, "He doesn't know. He can't know. And if he does know, we'll deny it."

Debbie said, "I wonder if it would have worked if we used the 'Konig, Konig' chant?"

Verna said, "*I* really didn't do anything."

Iris and I were the last ones through the door. The room looked exactly the same, except this time it was full of Uncle Otto. He was sprawled across the bed with his taped right leg propped up on a pillow. "Girls," he boomed, "I'm going to make this very brief. I know you've got to get to Evening Activity. What is it tonight?"

"A movie," Verna said, " 'Operation Pacific', with John Wayne."

"Well, you'll want to get to the movie. I just want to say that, since this little accident, I've had some time to think; and I've thought a lot about some of you girls. I believe that I may have been a little too harsh with you."

I closed my eyes.

He continued, "Parents' Weekend is a very hectic time, especially for those of us behind the scenes who have to see to it that things run smoothly. I might have lost my temper too quickly, and I apologize for that. Iris? I can't see you."

Adele and Debbie moved quickly to either side, leaving Iris up front.

"Iris, I'm not excusing the fact that you disappeared, leaving a lot of worried people. But I may have been too strict in punishing you. I'm taking back that punishment as of now and we'll say no more about it. That's all, go to your movie."

Everybody just turned and filed out. Except me.

"Uncle Otto?"

"Yes?"

"I hope you feel better."

26

"Iris is going to play her guitar in the musicale
Thursday night," I said after the lights were out.

"No, I'm not."

"You are! She is!"

"That's a neat idea," Adele said. "Do 'Leavin' on
a Jet Plane'. I love that."

"No, do 'Dylan's Dream'," Nat said.

" 'Blue Frog'!" Debbie yelled.

"I'm not playing," said Iris.

"You have to. You're better than anyone," I said,
"and we'll all sing with you. I promised!"

"Oh, *yes!*" Nat said.

"Oh, no!" Iris said.

"Iris, just tell us why, when you can do something so well, you don't want anyone to know about
it," I said.

No answer."

"Iris," I whispered, "please do it. Do it for *me*.
Do it for *you*. But please, *please* play. Everyone

will love it. Our bunk will be so proud." Iris still didn't answer. I figured I'd better drop it. I could start again in the morning and, if I nagged enough, I'd wear her down. It always worked with Mom. Nobody nags like I nag.

The next morning reveille blew over the loudspeaker at the same time Verna's alarm went off. "Verna, you didn't have to set your alarm," Debbie grumbled. "Uncle Otto won't be yelling for a while and we can wake up to the bugle."

"Well, I didn't want to take any chances," Verna said.

Just before Line-Up I started again. "Iris?"

"Don't start, Tuffy!" she said.

"Iris, I'm not going to be able to stand it if you don't play tomorrow night." She shook her head and went out to Line-Up.

But I wasn't the only one nagging. Natalie came up to me and pushed me ahead of the others. "Well, Tuf, have you thought about our next trick?"

"What next trick?"

"*You* know, the next spell we're going to work. I've thought a lot about it, and I've got some terrific ideas."

"Natalie, I don't want to think about that now."

"Look, Tuffy, you have a magic touch. You're the one who can make it work. Listen, we can do anything we want. And boy, do I want!"

I walked away from Nat and stood next to Iris. As soon as the flag came down, I said, "Iris?"

"All right, Tuffy."

"What?"

"I said, 'all right,' I'll do it."

"Uh, terrific! How come?"

"Because the thought of you bugging me every ten minutes for two entire days is worse than anything that could happen to me on a stage!"

We all fought during the entire Rest Hour over what songs we should do.

"Let's do 'Sunshine'," Debbie said. "I love that!"

" 'Tie a Yellow Ribbon'," Adele said.

"How about 'Boogie Fever?" Natalie suggested.

"Boo," said Verna.

"The folk songs sound better," I said.

" 'Bad, Bad Leroy Brown'," yelled Nat.

"Wait a minute, everybody's talking at once," Verna said, taking out her stationery and a pen. "I'll write down the songs we all want and then we'll narrow it down."

" 'Jimmy Crack Corn'," Debbie said, loudly.

"NO!" from Nat.

"Will you just wait a minute?" Verna said. "I'm writing. 'Jimmy . . . ' "

"Not that," Natalie insisted. "Let's do 'This Land Is Your Land'."

"I like that," Adele said.

" 'Dylan's Dream'," I offered.

"Oh, yes!" said Nat.

Verna was writing like crazy. "Look," she said, "let's organize this. We'll go around the beds and each girl say one song."

"You can skip me," Iris put in, "I like all the songs I play. I don't care which ones you pick."

We went around the beds five times and came up with twenty-five songs. We were about to go around again when Debbie asked, "Hey! how many do we need, anyway?"

"Two," I answered.

"TWO??" It was a chorus.

"Uh, yeah, but with a third 'possible'."

"You mean," Nat said, "that we've got to narrow down twenty-five songs to *three?*"

"Uh huh."

"Oh, great! How are we going to do that?"

"I have an idea," Verna said, "we'll put all the songs into a hat and pick out three."

"Good," Adele said.

Verna began to cut out the song titles that she had written. When she was finished, we put them into Debbie's bunny cap. "Who'll pick?" Nat asked.

"I will," Verna said.

"You can't," Nat said. "You wrote them. You'll recognize them."

"How could I recognize twenty-five pieces of paper?" Verna yelled.

"Someone else has to do it," Natalie insisted.

"I'll pick!" I said.

"Not you, Tuffy. You'll put a magic spell on them and pick the ones you want," Nat said.

"Natalie, you're really crazy."

"I'll do it myself," said Nat.

"*I* will," Debbie said.

"Let Iris pick," I finally said. "That'll be the fairest, since she doesn't care which songs we sing."

Everyone agreed.

We all cheered when the first song Iris pulled out of the cap was "Scarborough Fair." That's a beautiful song. Then she picked "Jimmy Crack Corn."

"Ohhhhh, no!" Nat said. "I'm not singing 'Jimmy Crack Corn.' I sang that when I was five."

"It's a good song, Nat," Iris said, "its fun. All the little kids will like that and it's something the whole camp knows. We can get up and walk through the audience and get everyone to sing."

"Get her," Nat said, "this morning that guitar wasn't leaving the bunk. Now she's a strolling minstrell"

"No, it's a good idea," Adele said. "Iris is right. The first song is kind of sad, and this one is happy and jumpy. The whole camp will sing 'Jimmy Crack Corn'."

"Paul never sings 'Jimmy Crack Corn'," Natalie said.

"Which is exactly why *we* should," I said. "Pick one more, Iris, in case they just won't let us off the stage."

"A star is born," Natalie said.

Iris picked "John Henry", and nobody had a bad word to say about that.

We rehearsed for the rest of that day and all the next, Thursday, the day of the musicale. Natalie made a face each time she sang "Jimmy Crack Corn", but at least she sang.

We were going to be the eighth act, the last one before the intermission. Ann, the Drama Counselor, didn't even audition us. All we did was tell her the songs we were going to sing, and I guess she figured they were okay.

We had an enormous argument over what to wear. It started at dinner, continued during Free Play and was still going on when it was almost time to go to the Rec Hall. We all thought we should dress alike, but we couldn't agree on the proper outfit. Finally we decided *not* to dress alike. Everyone would wear what *she* wanted to wear and that would be it . . . So we all wore jeans.

"Are you nervous, Iris?" Debbie asked. I jabbed her in the ribs.

"No," Iris said.

We waited backstage until our group was announced. Ann said, "And now, here's Bunk Ten." That's what you call a really warm introduction! We walked out and grouped ourselves around Iris. It took a minute to tune up and get us all in the right key, but we made it. "Scarborough Fair" was one big hit! No one talked, everybody listened and applauded like crazy when we were finished. I could see Alex sitting with the Senior Boys, right in the middle. He was smiling. Was he smiling at me? They were still applauding when Iris launched right into "Jimmy Crack Corn." And she had been so right about that song! The littlest kids were stomping their feet and singing. When Iris got up and walked off the stage, right up the aisle still playing, with us following, everybody clapped their hands in rhythm and sang out loud! After about forty choruses, we'd had it! We went to our regular seats for intermission and the rest of the show. But the kids wanted Iris to play some more, and they shouted until she stood up. When she did, they cheered. She looked at the rest of us and motioned for us to follow.

As Debbie stood up to follow her, I clamped my arm down across her lap. "What's the matter?" she whispered loudly.

"Don't get up," I said. "Pass it on." So the five of us stayed in our seats. Iris, who was already up and couldn't do anything about it, shook her head and her fist at us. Then she got on that stage and wailed the heck out of "John Henry."

When the musicale was over, practically the whole camp went over to Iris to congratulate her . . . Campers, counselors, everybody! Iris's face was all red, and she was smiling a lot. I had such a good time watching her. I only wished Sheila could have seen it. At least Uncle Otto was there, sitting in the back with his foot propped up on Aunt Louise.

When we got back, Natalie was the last one in the bunk. She slammed the door behind her. "All *right,*" she said, sounding like an army sergeant, "now that that's over, it's time to concentrate on other things. I think we ought to get back to what we started, testing our magic powers. Personally, I'd like to have Tuffy make a love potion, but I'm willing to wait for that. First, I think we should try a spell for everyone, to make absolutely sure it works, even though we've proven that it does."

"I know," Debbie said, "why not put a spell on

the cook and have him make every meal a Parents' Weekend meal!"

"How about a spell to cure my allergies?" Adele asked. "Then you'll be a real Jonas Salk, Tuf!"

"How about a spell to go to sleep?" I muttered.

"Come on, Tuf!" Natalie was as big a nag as I was. "This time we won't hurt anyone. Honest! It'll be a nice spell."

"G'night, Nat."

"Think about it, Tuf."

When the lights were finally out and everyone was quiet, I leaned over toward Iris's bed.

"Are you still up?" I whispered.

"Yes."

"Are you angry at me?"

"What for?"

"For leaving you up there on the stage alone."

She didn't answer for a long time. I thought maybe she hadn't heard me. Finally she said, "You know, I would have been angry if it had happened a few weeks ago, but not now. I know why you did it, and I couldn't be angry with you."

Okay, I thought, O-kay!

27

I spent the next few days avoiding Natalie. She really thought she could make everything terrific through magic, and she wouldn't leave me alone. "You made it work, Tuffy," she kept insisting. "There's nothing you can't do!"

I thought about it a lot. And what I thought about mostly was why I didn't want to do it. If this had happened last winter . . . If Natalie had asked me at the beginning of the summer . . . I would have done anything! I would have loved it. Maybe I'd even be famous. After all, it was easy. But now . . . Maybe it *was* a freaky coincidence. Maybe it didn't work at all. Could I take a chance and try it again? Maybe it's like bowling, where you always get a strike the first time you throw the ball but never after that, unless you practice. But what if somebody got hurt? I just didn't know.

Rest Hours and nights were the worst. Debbie started in with Natalie. Even Adele got buggy.

"Tuffy, just do some little thing. Some dumb thing! Anything!" Natalie nagged. "You've got the power, so use it!"

"Try it, Tuffy," Adele said. "How about if we just do some funny thing, like having the whole camp oversleep tomorrow morning? Look up a sleeping spell."

"Please," I said, putting my hands over my ears.

"Will you all knock it off?" Iris said. "She doesn't *want* to!"

"Hey, Iris," Adele said, "you try it."

"Yes," Natalie jumped in, "you're the one with the books. You could do it just as well as Tuffy."

"*You're* the one who said the whole thing was so interesting," Debbie added. "Now, just when everyone else is interested too, you won't play."

"Don't you want to experiment?" Adele asked.

"No," said Iris.

"I don't believe you," Natalie persisted.

Iris just looked from one to the other as they talked. The more she didn't answer, the more they pleaded. Finally, she couldn't stand it anymore. "Stop!" she shouted suddenly. She picked up her pillow and hugged it to her chest. Tears started in her eyes. "You think I can work magic!" she cried. "You think I can make magic happen? *Listen* to me." Everyone shut up as her voice got lower and hoarser. "Do you know how many years I've been at boarding school? Six. *Six* years, and I'm only twelve years old. If I'm lucky, I get to see my parents at Thanksgiving. I never see them at Christmas, because Christmas is the time they go skiing at Sun Valley. One time they took me with them—" She was crying—"but I was too young to ski with them, so I spent Christmas vacation on the kiddy slopes with some ski instructor."

"A ski instructor?" Nat asked.

"Shut up, Nat," I said.

"On my summer vacations I visit my aunt at her ranch in Arizona or I go to—to camp!" She wiped her face on the pillow and hugged it harder. "Sure, I read a lot about the supernatural because I just couldn't think of any other way I could get noticed in my own house unless it was *by magic!*" She started to yell and, through her tears, her voice got shrill. "But here I am! I'm here, at camp *again!* And I leave for school on the day after Labor Day! So you think I can work magic? Do you think I'd be here if I could?" She got up off her bed. Still clutching her pillow, she fled out the door, leaving us all sitting there with our mouths open.

After a little while, I went outside. She was curled up with her pillow at the far end of the porch. I sat down and leaned against the bunk wall.

"Hey, I've got an idea," I said.

Her face was buried in the pillow but she said, "What?"

"If you don't have to go back to school until Labor Day, we could meet in the city and go to a concert or something."

She came up out of the pillow. "Do you think the Schaefer Music Festival will still be running in Central Park when we get home?"

"Gee, I don't know. Does it go through Labor Day?"

"Well, it's been getting longer every year. Wouldn't it be great if Joni Mitchell were playing somewhere!"

"Or Phoebe Snow."

"Yeah."

"Listen, Iris, if your folks aren't around at vacation time, you could spend it at my house. We could do lots of neat things."

Iris put down her pillow. "I'd really like that."

"Yeah, but meanwhile, there'll be other neat things to do," I said.

"Like what?"

"Well, toward the end of camp, they always have a camp sing. Didn't your other camp have one?"

"Yeah, they did."

"Well, the songs are always written by the campers. Wouldn't you like to do that? We take tunes that we already know and put new words to them."

"We did that, too!" she said. "And one of the songs was supposed to be funny, where you sang a verse about every counselor in camp."

"Yeah! And sometimes they were zingers!"

"But funny," she said.

"Oh, of course! Do you know the song 'Louise'?"

Iris thought. "You mean the one that goes 'Every little breeze seems to whisper Louise'?"

"Right. Well how do you like this for Aunt Louise, since she's always up at the infirmary?" I sang:

"Every little sneeze seems to whisper Louise
Kids with a wheeze seem to sniffle Louise."

Iris laughed. "Let's see if I can add to it." She
thought a minute. "How's this?

Each stuffy nose tells me it
Grows to love you, Louise."

"Fantastic!" I screamed. We both laughed. "Let's
volunteer to write the whole thing!"

"The whole thing! Are you kidding?" Iris said,
but she smiled.

I looked out across the Quad. It was empty except for one boy, walking with his head down and
carrying a small suitcase. "Hey, just a minute," I
said to Iris and got up. It was Alex. He slowed
down when he saw me walking toward him.

"Are you running away?" I asked, nodding toward the suitcase.

"Nah! I'm going to the infirmary. I've got the
measles."

"Wow, you sure do!" I laughed, looking at his
face. "Okay, I'm sorry I laughed. It's not funny.
How long does it take to get rid of the measles?"

"Just a few days, I hope." He started walking
away.

"Didn't you have the shot?"

"I thought I did," he answered. "Maybe it didn't
work."

"It's probably the kind you can't get a shot for.
German measles. That's very mild."

"Good."

"Got anything to read in the suitcase?"

"Aw, no, I forgot. I just grabbed pajamas, tooth-brush, that junk."

"I'll get you some comics and magazines." I turned and ran back to the bunk. "Talk to you later," I said, waving at Iris. "I want to get some stuff for Alex." I had a bunch of stuff to read in my cubby, *Sports Illustrated*, Spiderman and Archie comics, a book of Alfred Hitchcock mysteries, and three science fiction magazines . . . my mother's into science fiction. I was throwing them into a bag, when Nat came up to me.

At first I thought she was going to apologize, but instead she was mad. "Some friend you are, Tuf! All I ask is one little favor from you the whole summer. Didn't I help you when you wanted to make the doll?"

"Listen, Natalie," I said quietly, "I'm sorry, I really am. But I'm just not interested in that stuff anymore. So leave me alone."

Natalie glared at me. "Hens don't have teeth, anyway," she snorted.

I picked up the bag of books and started toward the infirmary. On the way, I passed Uncle Otto's cabin. He was outside, sitting in a lounge chair with his bandaged foot propped up on a stool.

"Hi," I said.

He looked at me and nodded. "Hello, Tuffy."

"How's your foot?"

"Better, thank you."

"You're welcome."

I swung the bag over my shoulder and continued on up to the infirmary. The doctor stopped me at the door and told me that Alex was not allowed any visitors. So I walked around to the back and started whispering his name under every window.

I got an answer from a window at the corner.

"Hi," I said. "I brought you some stuff, but they won't let me in."

"No sweat," he said at the window. "I'll slice open the screen with a nail file."

I couldn't reach the window with the bag so I had to go hunting for a rock to stand on.

"Hey, good stuff. Thanks a lot," he said, when we got the bag inside.

"You're welcome. How do you feel?"

"I feel fine," he said, "but itchy."

"Maybe it's not the measles. Maybe it's poison ivy or something."

"Poison ivy wouldn't spread like this. Besides, I have a temperature."

"Oh. Gee, that's too bad." I sat down on my rock.

"Yeah. Man, this is going to be boring," he said.

"Well, I'll come back and see you during Free Play. I'll knock on the wall right under your window, like this." I knocked softly two times. "If someone's there, knock back and I'll get away fast."

"Okay."

"Do you want anything else?"

"Nah."

"Well, I guess I'd better be getting back. So long." I started to walk away.

"Hey, Tuffy!"

"What?"

He cocked his head and smiled at me. "What's your real name, anyway?"

I smiled back. "Elizabeth," I said.

Judy Blume

Judy Blume <u>knows</u> about growing up. She has a knack for going right to the heart of even the most secret problems and feelings. You'll always find a friend in her books—like these from Laurel-Leaf!

PAULA DANZIGER